THE NIGHT SILVER RIVER RUN RED

CHRISTINE MORGAN

DEATH'S HEAD PRESS

an imprint of Dead Sky Publishing, LLC
Miami Beach, Florida
www.deadskypublishing.com

ISBN: 9781639510405

Cover Art: Justin T. Coons

The "Splatter Western" logo designed
by K. Trap Jones

Book Layout: Lori Michelle
www.TheAuthorsAlley.com

Part One:
After Dark

1

RISKING A WHIPPING

SOME THINGS, Cody claimed, were worth risking a whipping.

Emmett surely did hope so, because this, if they got caught, meant the kind of whipping so as to make a boy's sit-upon unfit for sitting-upon the rest of the week.

It'd be like that for him, anyways.

For him, just having sneaked out so late would mean a whipping. Let alone sneaking out with Cody and Mina, since their pa and his didn't get along on the best of days. Of course, Emmett's pa didn't get along with most anybody, except for Preacher Gaines and Mayor Fritt. And even then, it was only on the surface. At home, behind closed doors whilst railing to the captive audience of wife and son, Mr. Emmerson Pryce was like as not to refer to the preacher as a God-thumper no better than those crazy heathen Truthers up in Highwell, and the mayor as a puffed-up fool on the verge of letting the whole town dry up and blow away. He certainly had no patience for Mr. McCall, Cody and Mina's pa, who'd been a range rider and bounty hunter before a gunshot injury forced him to settle down and take over running the post office. Nor did he approve of Mrs. McCall, their ma, fancying herself all educated, looking to start up a newspaper.

No sir, sneaking out with Cody and Mina was asking for trouble. And, throwing Albert into the mix? Albert and his family, who run the livery stables, being what politer folks around Silver River called 'colored' and all?

Emmett's bottom fair to burned just thinking about it. Taking his meals standing up, having to choose between scoldings from stern Miz Abigail for squirming on the painful-hard schoolhouse benches or enduring the shame of bringing a cushion . . . not to mention the occasional smack to the backside so as to assure he hadn't forgotten . . .

He knew all that, knew it heart-close and well. Yet, here he was all the same, out here in Starkey's woodlot, the four of them picking their way through the moonlit darkness with just Mina's little hooded lantern and Albert's occasional matchsticks to help them along.

It was a shortcut, Cody had said. Straight across, hardly more than a mile, and they'd be to Lost Meadow. *Then* they'd see what they would see, right enough! Well worth risking a whipping! *Well* worth it, for a mighty temptation such as this!

Easy for him to say. Emmett doubted Cody ever got much of a whipping. Like as not, his pa would grin, tousle Cody's sandy hair, and give him a nip of whiskey instead. At most, he'd earn himself a wrist-slap or a tut-tut for letting his baby sister tag along on the night's adventure . . . and even that, Emmett doubted. Mina McCall was willful to say the least. If Cody hadn't let her tag along, she would've followed on her own.

Now and again, Emmett's pa would grouse to his ma that maybe they ought to pack up and leave, go someplace where 'the boy' could have a better caliber of associates and influences. Silver River was dying, anyway. Soon be no better than the hundreds of other ghost towns where the veins petered out, boom gone to bust.

To think, not so very long ago, there'd been a whole thriving mining camp, with talk of the railroad building in! Emmett could still remember the hardpacked lanes thick with wagons and stagecoaches, new businesses rising every day like sunflowers in a field, noisy evenings when prospectors would come in from their claims to spend their earnings—no gold, true, but a rich silver strike was nothing to be sneezed at—in the saloons and lady-houses.

These days, but a single saloon held on, the Silver Bell. The lady-houses, which Emmett wasn't supposed to know about, had all closed, the ladies seeking greener pastures elsewhere. The proposed railroad plans had fell through. There weren't hardly more than a dozen places left open in the downtown, though the surrounding farmlands were doing fine and dandy. Silver River may have run out of silver, but it hadn't run out of river.

Be barely able to keep up a living here soon, Emmett's pa had said. When there'd been claim disputes, theft, fighting, and so on, there'd been work aplenty for a lawyer. His days had been so full with cases, making ready for the circuit judge's visits, he'd scarce had time to bother with his wife and son. Didn't raise his voice, or his hand, to them as long as dinner was on the table and they made presentable for church every Sunday.

But, bit by bit, it dwindled away. Less and less work for a lawyer. More and more time to stew in his study, find fault with his wife's cooking and housekeeping, with his son's marks at school and diminishing circle of reputable age-mate friends.

Now, there were just Emmett, Cody, and Albert. All the other boys around were either old enough to be considered nearly men full-grown, too young to be good for much besides playing stick-ball and kick-can in the streets, or still clinging to their mommas' aprons.

As for girls their age, well, there was Lizzie Cottonwood, whose rancher pa was the wealthiest landholder between here and Winston City, but Lizzie cared more for dresses and bonnets and the like than for adventures. The mayor's twin nieces weren't much better. Daisy-Ann Dunnings was all right, but with her pa bein' drunk and her ma bein' sickly, she had the care of her little siblings more often than not.

That left Mina McCall, three years younger than Cody and Emmett's thirteen, a year younger than Albert.

So, they were four, whispering in the woodlot's secret rustling dark. Four, alive with the rules-breaking thrill of the forbidden. And it didn't matter none if Albert were colored, if Mina were only a girl, if Emmett were on the scrawny side and sometimes stuttered when he spoke. It didn't matter none, because Cody was with them, brash and dash enough to make up for them all.

"Is that where we're going?" asked Mina, nodding in the direction of a distant dim-lit window-square to the north.

"Nah, that's the Starkey place," Cody said. "We'll steer clear of there, he's as apt as not to set his dogs on us."

"I like dogs," said Mina.

"Not these ones, you wouldn't." Big-brotherly, he turned toward her and loomed with a monstrous pose and toothy smile. "Size of ponies, they are, ugly as bristly boar-hogs, with jaws like bear-traps."

Emmett and Albert glanced nervously at the distant window-light, but Mina stuck out her tongue and rude-noised in response. "I ain't scared."

Cody chuckled. "Better not be, not with what we're gonna see!" He patted his shirt pocket, where folded paper crinkled. "Wonders and horrors, my friends, like we ain't never imagined!"

"My brother Abram says Lacy Cavanaugh's the only whore left in Silver River," Albert said.

They all looked at him. Cody whooped a loud laugh, stifling it quick. "Oh yeah? What's Abram know about that?"

"Miz Lacy's a what?" Mina asked.

"He s-said '*hor-ror*'," Emmett enunciated, struggling not to blush. "As in, frightening-like."

"Oh."

"No, go on, tell us!" Cody nudged Albert. "Your brother been keepin' time with Miz Lacy? Late hours at the Bell?"

"Now, wait, Abram would never—"

"What's wrong with Miz Lacy?" Mina persisted. "I like her. She plays cards and drinks whiskey and rides stride-saddle—"

Cody whooped again and slapped his thigh a loud whack. "I *bet* she does!"

"Sssst," hissed Emmett. "Want Starkey's d-dogs to hear?"

"Right, right." He again muffled himself. "Surprised we ain't already heard them barkin' up a storm. C'mon. We'd best step a move on. Gettin' late. Mina, raise up that lamp. Yeah. This-a-way."

He resumed leading. They hadn't gone but twenty paces before they did hear a snarling volley of rough barks, and froze in their tracks. Emmett could all too readily imagine pony-sized bear-trap boar-hogs crashing through the underbrush. He'd seen animals Starkey's mongrels had gotten at, what was left of them, anyways. Hares, barn cats, even coyotes, reduced to bloodied rag-scraps of fur and hide, guts and gristle. Once, a prize calf had wandered off the Cottonwoods' ranch and run afoul of the pack. Got itself butchered seven ways to Sunday. That had brought his pa a nice case to wrangle, though it certainly had not endeared the Pryces to Old Man Starkey.

Baying devil-hounds did not, however, come barreling at them from the tree-shadows, muzzles wire-bristled with fangs and tusks, ready to rend apart their tender young flesh into quivering pink lumps of meat. Instead, the rough barking ended in an abrupt, pained, glottal yelp . . . a gurgling whimper

. . . then silence.

"Reckon someone risked a whippin', at that," Cody said.

Mina frowned. "Did he hurt the dog?"

"Wouldn't surprise me none," Albert muttered.

"Me, neither," Emmett said. "Maybe this isn't such a good idea. Maybe we should turn b-back."

"Oh, now, don't," Cody said. "We're almost to Lost Meadow. All this way, and you want to go home before we catch us a glimpse?" He patted his pocket again. "You seen these handbills, same as me, I know you have. Posted all over town. Din't the fancy-man bring one to your pa's office week-a'forelast?"

"He d-did . . . " Emmett had been perched at the clerk's desk in the file room, laboring over his sums under his pa's merciless scrutiny—following an unsatisfactory report from Miz Abigail the schoolmarm—when the fancy-man had come in.

And, lordy, hadn't he *been* a fancy one! Trousers of what looked like black velvet, glossy black leather boots, snow-white high-collar shirt, shiny sateen vest of emerald green, a matching dandy green cap tilted rakishly atop slicked-back jet-black hair, watch-chain and cuff-links twinkling gold! His eyes had been likewise green, likewise twinkling. A beaming smile had shone bright through boyish, dimpled cheeks as the fancy-man strode bold-as-billy up to Mr. Pryce, extending a hand while launching into his speech.

Rapid-patter though the fancy-man spoke, he only got a few sentences in before Mr. Pryce had silenced him with a raised stop-palm and a glowering look.

" . . . and my pa would have none of it," Emmett continued. "Said Silver River might be on its last legs but was still too fine a town for traveling trash. Wouldn't let him post a handbill in the window. Told him to try his luck in Winston City or some other place without decent m-morals."

"Traveling *trash*?" Cody echoed. "It's a circus, is all! A show!"

"A *freak*-show," Albert added, kind of under his breath, but Cody heard him anyways.

"A carnival of oddities and museum of marvels. Says so right here!" He pulled the oft-folded paper from his pocket and unfolded it along its creases, tilting it into the modest spill of lantern-light.

Printed on it, in large and ornate garish lettering, were those very words: ***DOCTOR ODDICO'S CARNIVAL OF ODDITIES AND MUSEUM OF MARVELS!***

Along the page's edges ran columns of grainy poster-style illustrations, the space in between filled with more words:

SHIVER at the Pallid Countenance of the Living Ghost!

BEHOLD Tom Short, the World's Smallest Negro!

CONSULT the All-Knowing Mother Sybil!

STAND AGOG before the Mighty Man-Mountain!

WITNESS the Lethal Arts of the Deadly Lotus!

WONDER at the Uncanny Aim of the Blind Bandito!

BE AWESTRUCK by Princess Crow-Feather's Bird Magic!

Below those was an additional invitation to **Tour the Ten-In-One Gallery of Grotesqueries**, and the announcement of a *Free Bonus Attraction: Exhibits of the Exotic!*

At the bottom of the page, in spaces deliberately left blank after a printed **When** and a **Where**, someone had handwritten in times and dates for the upcoming Friday and Saturday, as well as "Lost Meadow Campground, Silver River Valley."

However often he read it, Emmett couldn't deny a giddy prickle of excitement. He had vague memories of, as a much smaller boy, his ma and pa taking him to a traveling circus-show that'd come through, with trick riders and tumblers and juggler-clowns—and more vivid memories of eating too much fried sweetdough and spun-sugar candy and sicking up all over his pa's shirtfront, and how furious his pa had been—but nothing much of the sort had happened around town in years. The occasional singer or storyteller might happen by, and a troupe of actors one winter put on a Christmas play in the livery's hay-barn, but otherwise, visiting entertainment was few and far between.

But, visiting entertainment the likes of this? Oddities, marvels, grotesqueries? Bird-magic? A living ghost? Deadly arts? Oh, Preacher Gaines might have waxed righteous in church the past two Sundays about it, but from what Emmett had sensed, most of his decrying of such wickedness had only fueled the fires of interest. Besides, it made a break from his usual decryings of the heretic Truthers and lecturing on temperance and temptation.

Thinking of which, temperance and temptation that was, rumor did have it the fancy-man had gone to great pains to assure Mr. Harlowe at the Silver Bell that there'd be no such competition for the saloon's business. Or Miz Lacy's, for that matter. Doctor Oddico's show offered no drinking, no gambling, no scantily-clad dancing girls, nothing of the sort. In fact, the fancy-man was reputed to have said, their company welcomed—nay, relished!—cooperative efforts with local establishments, and if Mr. Harlowe was so inclined as to run a whiskey-cart out to Lost Meadow for those evenings, agreeable arrangements certainly could be made. Likewise for the Moss sisters, who had the general store, or Mr. and Mrs. Gillins at the bakery, if they cared to. Why, if someone from Nan's Cookpot wanted to set up a stall, why not? Make an event of it! Make a full proper fair of it!

The fancy-man—Sebastian Farstairs, as he'd introduced himself to Emmett's pa—indeed had quite the charm about him, and it'd served him well at most other businesses around Silver River. He'd had those handbills posted in almost every shop window before the day was out.

The show had been the talk of the town ever since, Silver River buzzing like a bee-hive with anticipation.

Then, according to the men who fence-rode Cottonwoods' ranch, yesterday afternoon the company had been sighted rolling in. A mismatched wagon-train hodge-podge if ever there was one, they said. Colorful, though, even before tents and banners started going up. None of them had ridden over for a closer look, merely watching from afar. But even that was enough to confirm one of the handbill's promises.

"Fella must've been seven, eight foot tall if he was an inch," had gone the word at Nan's Cookpot over supper that evening. "Broad as two bulls and hairy as a grizzly. Their 'Man-Mountain,' gotta be. Looked like he could twist a body's head off easy as an apple off the stem."

If he even *was* a man, further speculation went. Everyone had heard tell of the hulking forest brutes seen up Oregon way, after all. There were those giant gorilla-apes captured in Africa, too; Miz Abigail had a science book with genuine photographs. And didn't some of the local savage tribes have legends of braves turning into giant bear-man warriors?

This morning had brought another tantalizing development, when fancy-man Sebastian Farstairs rode back into town, accompanied by two others.

One was a woman of severe Oriental beauty, clad neck-to-toes in form-fitting black leather—no skirt or dress for her, but trousers tight as a coat of paint!—and she outright bristled with weapons. Sheathed swords, slimmer than cavalry sabers, crossed her back. Belts of knives, daggers, and curved hook-blades girded her narrow waist, upper arms, and lean thighs. Two more daggers, long and thin, pierced the knotted bun of her hair. Her slanted ebony eyes were like blades themselves, sharp, and cold.

The other rider appeared to be a man, but it was hard to tell, given the enveloping hooded cloak and robe of deep scarlet covering everything except hands gloved and feet booted in the softest, supplest kidskin. All that could be seen within the crimson confines of the hood was the hint of a pale blur that might've been a masked face.

Or, as the handbill said, perhaps *the Pallid Countenance of the Living Ghost*? While, possibly, the woman's weaponry indicated *the Lethal Arts of the Deadly Lotus*?

Neither of them spoke, simply rode in silence alongside the fancy-man. He, however, spoke enough for all three. His trained voice rang from one end of the main street to the other as, with many a flourish and gesture, he thanked Silver River for their hospitality and expressed how delighted he and Doctor Oddico's entire company were at the prospect of welcoming such good people to join them on Friday or Saturday evening. Or both! Some wonders had to be seen twice to be believed!

As an extra incentive, he scattered around a fistful of free passes to the *Gallery of Grotesqueries*, where, he promised, those souls brave enough to enter would be greeted with 'ten unthinkable abominations, forever preserved in all their hideous splendor!' Oh, people fair to clamored and pushed and shoved to get hold of one!

Emmett had watched the entire thing from his bedroom window, nose squashed to the glass. He heard his pa downstairs, growling something about how anybody fool enough to go to that show deserved whatever they got . . . and hoping someone *did* get hurt so he could bring a case against those degenerates.

As if he hadn't already guessed as much, Emmett knew asking to go was well out of the question. To further hammer the point home, his own pa joined forces with Preacher Gaines and Miz Abigail, the three of them browbeating Mayor Fritt into making a declaration that only those age of fifteen or older would be allowed to attend, for it was clearly no fit thing for children.

Or for decent ladies of quality, Miz Abigail added, with the swift support of Emmett's ma and most of the other wives and female members of Preacher Gaines' flock. Lacy Cavanaugh knew better than to chime in her thoughts, though the Moss sisters—tough old spinsters who'd taken on the general store when their pa died and their no-good nephew run off—weren't about to let 'church mice and mother geese' tell *them* what to do.

Mrs. McCall, Cody and Mina's ma, announced meanwhile it'd be a grand story for her newspaper, though she did with some reluctance agree it might be best to keep the youngsters at home . . . Friday, at least, so as to give parents the opportunity to judge for themselves.

A person might think, and Emmett certainly had, that this would've been enough for Cody; once his ma went on Friday, she'd be bound to grant him permission to go on Saturday. Heck, Mina too, and their pa. Whole family might go, Mayor Fritt and his declaration be damned.

But, far as Cody was concerned, it wasn't enough. On the off chance his ma decided against it, he quick-like hatched a plan to sneak out for a look-see and put it before his friends that very afternoon.

Albert had agreed with no hesitation. A whipping, he explained, was not a risk he had to worry over. "My granpappy told us our folk done been whipped enough in years past to last for generations t'come. B'sides, a *we ain't mad, we's just disappointed* look from my momma's punishment enough."

This, also, Emmett doubted, and on some inner level felt a grudge how, really, only *he* was risking an actual whipping, then, but he held his peace and let it go. Not like his pa needed an excuse, anyhow. An undercooked steak with so much as a blush of pink still in it would send Mrs. Pryce to bed with fresh bruises, albeit carefully situated where her sleeves and collar made sure they didn't show. Why, even when a deceased relation back East left her a nice sum, which one might think should've pleased her husband, it seemed only to further stir his irritation.

In a strange logic, though, maybe if'n Emmett got his pa riled at *him* instead, it'd gain her a reprieve? Well, either way, here he was.

"We'll wait until after supper and bedtime," Cody had told them, "then meet up b'hind the livery, cut 'cross the lumberyard, and duck down Pigwaller Gulch. Clear shot to the woodlot with no one bein' the wiser."

So he'd said, so they'd done, and so far so good. With Mina, who'd overheard, insisting herself along for the ride. Just as well she did, since she was the one who thought to bring a lantern. Otherwise they'd've been making do in the dark woodlot with nothing but Albert's box of matchsticks and what moonlight filtered through the trees. Albert had also brought along a canteen, as well as some stale corn biscuits and dried apples to share around if they got hungry. Cody's own ideas of preparation included little more than a buck knife, the slingshot he'd named Deadeye, and a bag of river-pebbles. Emmett felt rather foolish for only making sure he had the clean kerchief he promised his ma he'd always carry, plus the usual boy-stuff of his pockets—a penny, a couple marbles, a snail shell, and a wooden whistle.

"From here, it's but a hop'n'skip," Cody said as they struggled up a slight rise littered with fallen branches. "Then we're at Lost Meadow to have ourselfs a peek."

"A peek at the freaks," muttered Albert, stooping to pick up a sturdy bough to serve in equal measures as walking stick or cudgel.

"Admit it, you want as much as any of us t'see what the Living Ghost's got under that hood, and if Man-Mountain's as big as they claim. And, hey, the World's Smallest Negro?"

"What, you think we all's know each other?"

"Don't'cha?"

"You know all white people?"

Cody pondered. "Huh. Well, when you put it thataway . . . "

Mina rude-noised again. "Cody Cornelius McCall, I swear, you are dumb as a stump sometimes. You sure you're older'n me?"

"Your middle name's C-Cornelius?" Emmett asked.

"Hell-*fire*, Mina, tell the world, why not!" As the others laughed, Cody added, "Was for our ma's granddaddy, ain't nothin' wrong with it!"

Past the top of the rise, the trees thinned out toward a straggle, and they emerged at the edge of Lost Meadow. In springtime, it bloomed bright with poppies and wildflowers, but just now with autumn coming on, the grasses were bent and heavy, high as Emmett's waist. Stalks whispered in a breeze like gossips in church.

Lost Meadow wasn't lost, was in fact right on the road what led from Silver River on up through the hills to Juniper—which really *had* become a ghost town—and on toward Winston City. Opinions varied on how it'd got its name, with the prevailing having to do with a homesteader family who'd simply vanished one deep winter, leaving all their things, a pot of beans frozen solid on the cold stove, livestock lowing half-starved in the shed.

Savage Indians, some claimed. Swept in, seized them all, scalped and skinned them, left the corpses for the coyotes. Went out in a blizzard, maintained others. Got separated looking for each other, snowblinded, went in circles calling and calling until they simply fell down dead. The ma done it, suggested yet others, ghoulishly; cabin fever took her, so's she poisoned her husband and young'uns and all. Or cooked and ate 'em, then hanged herself. Or the Devil come to their door and whisked them off to damnation.

No bones or bodies had ever been found, of course. Nor had the remains of any homesteader cabin, livestock shed, or frozen pot of beans. Wasn't hardly going to stop the talk. A few versions even had it that one member of the doomed family had survived, a baby boy left abandoned and not right in the head after all he'd witnessed . . . and that baby may or may not've grown up to become Old Man Starkey . . .

Whatever the truth, whether cursed or haunted or what, folk decided best to just leave it be and build elsewhere. If further proof was needed of the land's bad luck, why, guess where the hoped-for but fallen-through railroad line would've gone?

The Night Silver River Run Red

These days, the campground—a wide, cleared, rock-ringed patch near the road—was as close as anything came to a settlement at the spot. Freight haulers used it sometimes, carting loads of logs, coal, or quarried stone with their big slow ox-drawns. A detachment from Fort Winston might spend part of the summer doing trainings there, neat rows of white tents, booming cannons, brisk flags snapping in the wind.

For the most part, though, the space sat bare and undisturbed.

Now, however, was not for the most part. Now, however, a companionable jumble of mismatched wagons occupied the clearing. They were of many shapes and sizes, some drop-siders that'd fold open to make platforms, some like converted stagecoaches and high-rides, some good old covered Conestogas with canvas stretched taut over arching ring-hoops. Several blazing firepits shed enough illumination to hint at details of what, by full light of day, must've been a riot of paint and bright colors, decoration, poster-bills, and large cloth banner-signs.

Voices and laughter mingled with the sounds of a harmonica and what might've been a banjo or guitar. A dog, sounding much smaller than Starkey's brutes, yipped amiably. The scents of woodsmoke, coffee, fry-bread, and horse dung drifted on the air. The horses, themselves nearly as mismatched as the wagons they pulled, stood snuffing and chomping in a pen slapped together from pounded stakes strung with bob-wire.

Shadow-shapes of people moved hither and yon, though too far away to get a truly good look. All Emmett could tell with any certainty was that none of them appeared to be eight foot tall and broad as two bulls. Most looked normal enough: burly workhand-type men, a few women in ordinary dresses, a grey-haired colored man dishing up dinner, a black-braided girl maybe Mina's age playing fetch with the amiably-yipping dog, a shawl-wearing old lady busily knitting.

"Don't seem so freakish to me," Albert said. "And that best not be their notion of the World's Smallest Negro."

"Nah, must just be the cook," Cody said. "Let's get us closer. Quietly, now, and shutter the lamp."

Mina didn't move except to slow-reach one hand and tug at his sleeve, while staring wide-eyed in another direction altogether.

"What? I said, shutter the—" Cody turned and the rest of his words fell away unnoticed as fallen leaves. His eyes also went wide, and his mouth hung open like a sprung trap.

Emmett and Albert also turned, gasping together in surprise to find the four of them no longer alone.

2

SNEAK A PEEK

EMMETT'S HEART ABOUT hitch-locked in his chest, a hundred horrible thoughts stampeding through his mind.

It was the *Man-Mountain*, ready to twist their heads off their necks like apples off of stems!

It was Starkey's dogs, all boar-tusks and teeth, slavering to rip open their bellies and feast on their warm steaming guts!

It was the *Living Ghost*, whose *Pallid Countenance* would turn out to be a bleached and grinning empty-socketed skull!

It was mutilated homesteader corpses, scalped and skinned and heaved up from their shallow Lost Meadow graves!

It was the *Deadly Lotus*, more bristling with blades than a porcupine was with quills!

It was his angry pa, having followed and found him!

That last, and by far most likely, scared him so that he near to pissed his britches, a squirt-drop almost escaping before he realized none of the shapes standing before him belonged to his pa. Or, for that matter, to boar-tusked dogs, carnival freaks, or the restless murdered dead.

They were, instead, other children. Strangers, a girl and two boys, the girl maybe of an age with him and Cody, the boys somewhat younger.

Strangers, and . . . Truthers?

Truthers, sure enough! All three clad in those peculiar grey garments their kind wore, men and women alike—loose baggy trousers gathered by drawstrings at ankle and waist, shapeless grey over-smocks with likewise drawstring-cuffed sleeves, plain cloth shoes, floppy grey caps.

Emmett stared, feeling as agog as if he were looking square upon the carnival freaks. He'd never seen a Truther up this right close and personal before. Only ever on the rare occasions when some of them came down from Highwell, and even then, never youngsters. The few who did visit town, to trade honey-goods and flax and their odd-woven baskets at the general store, didn't stay long, just did their business and departed again. No tarrying at the Silver Bell or Nan's Cookpot, certainly no attending Sunday church.

His pa distrusted them mightily. Had, more than once—and with Preacher Gaines' full backing—suggested they be . . . encouraged . . . to move along. But Sheriff Travis would have none of it. *They're peaceful enough,* he'd say. *Cause no trouble, keep to themselves. So long as they abide by the law, they ain't doin' no harm.*

But, they're godless heathens, the preacher would

protest, *doing who knows what manner of pagan sacrifices up in the hills!*

They don't read or write or send their children for proper schooling, Miz Abigail often hastened to add.

What brought Mr. Pryce particular umbrage was how they didn't even *speak*, just held their solemn silence whilst watching folks in that secretive, knowing way that they had. Communicating by looks and gestures, in some unfathomable language of their own. Who knew what they could be saying? Or plotting? Rude, it was, he said. And sly. Worse than the Indians or the Chinee.

The sheriff always pointed out that the Truthers understood regular speech, read and wrote just fine, and *could* talk well as anybody. The one who most usually led the trade-errands to town—an older fella, prominently hook-nosed and bald as an egg beneath his floppy cap—spoke just fine, didn't he? Soft and low, but perfectly clear.

To this, the Moss sisters at the general store always agreed. Polite, he was, too, they said. Even when deflecting impertinent, nosy questions. Not a man for loose chatter, tale-telling, or idle gossip. Which, in their minds, put him a step above *some* around Silver River . . .

Emmett himself hadn't heard the bald Truther-man speak, hadn't ever been close enough. Whenever their somber grey forms appeared on the Highwell trail, trundling along their barrow-carts because they kept no horses, oxen, or ponies, he'd dutifully steer well clear, as his ma and pa had instructed. He'd only heard tell how each Truther wore a black flax-cloth band tied around his or her neck—though the bald man's was reputed to be bordered with white, as if a badge of his office granting him permission to use his voice in the presence of others. He'd only heard tell of their round upended basket-like houses, and the way they ate no meat. And the way Truther menfolk were said to share wives on account of how they hardly had any women, so their children might not even know who was their own pa.

This last tidbit was what most scandalized the ladies of Silver River. They, too, dutifully steered clear, pressing palms to their prim bodices as if to ward off being snatched from the street like in an Indian raid. This last tidbit, also, the Moss sisters scoffed at with great disdain. Cody and Mina's ma was likewise of a different mind, saying how maybe the rest of them were looking at it backwards, maybe it was Truther women had more freedom, and multiple husbands. Not like those folk up Utah way, where one man might hoard himself a whole bevy of wives. Oh, and did her opinions cause a tizzy? Best believe it!

"*Our* ma," Mayor Fritt's nieces had once told Cody at school recess, "says *your* ma is hellbound, same as Miz Lacy."

Overhearing which, Miz Abigail had not reprimanded them, but made a smug purse-lipped little nod. Lizzie Cottonwood, however, who seemed mighty sweet on Cody, took high offense and cut the twins dead from her social circle the full rest of the week. Not that Cody had noticed. He'd merely laughed and gone on slingshotting dented tin cans off the schoolyard fenceposts, nary a care in the world.

Lizzie Cottonwood, had she been here in Lost

Meadow this sneak-out night, would've been fit to split now if she saw the way Cody gawked at the Truther girl.

In fairness, Emmett and Albert gawked, too. Even Mina. But there was something different, something extra, in the way Cody did.

Even in those peculiar garments, even with her hair under the cap falling straight and smooth and cut off short in a razor's-edge line at the collarbones so it hung level with the black flax-cloth band around her throat, she was uncommon pretty. Skin like buttermilk. Hair like clover-honey fresh from the comb. Features fine as anything, with a slim nose, tapered chin, and clear brow.

And her eyes! They seemed almost too large for her face. Doe's eyes. Owl's eyes. Their exact color impossible to discern in Mina's lamplight, somewhere between molasses and whiskey-gold. Fringed with long, dark lashes . . . filled with the secretive, knowing Truther look that so infuriated Emmett's pa.

The boys, standing to each side and half-a-pace-or-so behind her, were identical in attire and similar in visage, though not nearly so pretty. Their hair was cropped bowl-cut at the length of their earlobes. One was more blondish, with a spatter of freckles across nose and cheeks. The other, more darkish, had a wider mouth slightly both gap- and buck-toothed.

The three Truthers, gawked at the Silver River kids with equal agog fascination. As if *their* clothing and hairstyles were what was *really* peculiar. As if they'd never seen the likes of a colored person up close, or Mina's calico dress, or Cody's scuffed hand-me-down boots.

It seemed a forever-span had passed, them all

staring at each other, but it must've been only a few breaths or so. The guitar, or banjo, over at the campground still plucked its same twangy tune, the dog still uttered its amiable yips.

"Uhhh . . . howdy," said Cody.

Both Truther-boys blinked their big owl-eyes as if startled. The girl regarded him a moment longer, then dipped her head in acknowledgment. Emmett noticed that none of them carried a lantern, or candle, or matchsticks. Could they, he wondered, see in the dark like owls as well? Like owls or like cats? How else could they have made their way through the woodlot, or down the narrow rocky crevice-ways from Highwell up in the hills?

The *how*, he might wonder, but the *why* quick proved plain enough—from a drawstring flax-cloth pursebag, the girl withdrew a folded and creased piece of familiar thick paper. She unfolded it and held it out to show them. A handbill, of course, same as were posted all over town. Same as what Cody had in his pocket. Grinning hugely, he removed his and showed it to her.

"Us too!" he said. "Come to sneak us a peek!"

"Shhh!" Emmett nudged him.

"Oh, yeah." In a hushed but exaggerated whisper, he repeated, "Us too!"

The Truther-girl smiled, and oh-gosh-and-Christmas . . . had he thought her uncommon pretty? Uncommon *beautiful*! Even Albert looked halfway to smitten, and Cody's evident admiration would've made Lizzie Cottonwood fair to foam at the mouth.

"Ain't none of you got no manners?" Mina stepped forward. "I'm Mina McCall, this here lummox is my brother Cody, this is Albert, and he's Emmett. What're your-all's names?"

"They can't tell you," Albert said. "They's Truthers, they can't talk."

"They *can*," Emmett put in. "They just d-don't, not to outsiders."

As one, they all three touched the black flax-cloth bands at their throats and nodded. But then, clearly shocking her companions even more than the rest, the girl reached behind her slender neck, unfastened a clasp, and drew the band away.

"My name is Saleel," she said.

Or something what sounded like that; Emmett wasn't full sure. Oh, but her voice, too, was like honey, slow and rich and sweet.

The Truther-boys, their big eyes half-popping from their heads, gesticulated wildly at her, looking around as if expecting some vengeful adult to descend. It somehow made him feel a bit better. A bit in common, as it were. Maybe for all that, they weren't so different after all. The girl, meanwhile—Saleel— gave them such a scoff as also needed no translation. They were in trouble enough already if'n they got caught, weren't they? that scoff said. What was a little more on top of that? In for a dime, in for a dollar . . . or whatever Truthers did for money.

"Sah-leel," Cody repeated, the careful way he did when Miz Abigail presented him with a new spelling word. "I'm Cody—"

"I done told her that, lummox," Mina cut in. She pushed forward, face bright with curiosity. "So, you really are Truthers? Tarnation! What's it like? I heard you don't eat meat? At all? Ever? Not even fried chicken? Fried chicken's just the best! What about bacon? You gotta eat bacon!"

"Unless they're like the Jewish," Albert said. "Jews don't eat bacon, ham, or any pork, near's I can recall."

"Oh, that's right . . . but, you ain't Jewish neither, are you? Preacher Gaines says you gots your own heathen gods—"

"M-mina!" gasped Emmett. "You can't just—"

"And what about your women havin' more'n one husband?" she pressed on. "How d'you know who your pa is? Or does it not matter?"

"Mina!" Cody managed some better than Emmett's wheezy squeak. "Hell-*fire*, and you said *I* ain't got no manners?"

She jutted a defiant chin. "Our ma would want me to ask! You know she's fair wild to know about their ways!"

"Yeah, but still, rein it in, girl!"

Throughout this, Saleel had followed the conversation intently, seeming to understand well enough. And to be amused by it, given her smile . . . which *was* right pretty, no question. The kind that made Cody stand himself up straight, even raking fingers through his hair in a token—if futile—attempt to tidy its tousled mess. Emmett imagined Lizzie Cottonwood at that moment springing bolt upright in her bed, like a goose had walked 'cross her grave.

Albert had gone on his tip-toes to peer toward the carnival camp. "Don't think they heard us," he said. "Seems the same over there. Washing up from dinner, and—holy horseshoes! Look!"

Everyone whirled to do so. Again, whatever their differences, in that moment they were each the same, jaw-dropped at the sight of what could only be the **Living Ghost**.

The figure striding past wagons still wore the crimson-red robe, but with the hood pushed back, so that firelight fell upon the advertised **Pallid Countenance**. Which was not a bleached-bone skull as Emmett had feared . . . but neither was it a matter of someone simply being fair-skinned or pale. He—this much was obvious, despite long loose-flowing locks of hair, was *white*.

White as fresh snow. White as summer clouds. White as the sculptures Miz Abigail had positioned on high shelves in the four corners of the schoolroom, busts of Presidents Washington, Jefferson, Lincoln, and Grant. Though, far more resembling those pictures of statues from ancient Rome or Greece or someplace than any of the depictions of those great men . . . flawless, unblemished, alabaster.

Even his hair, in its long loose-flowing locks more suited to a wealthy lady, was a startling-pure white. It glowed like the moon, which rode bright and full in the star-scattered black sky above.

"Well, how about that?" Cody whispered, after they'd watched him for a while. "What did I tell you?"

"He don't seem such a ghost, though," said Mina. "I mean, well, he's solid, ain't he? See? He just picked up that cup. He's drinkin' coffee. What kind of ghost would drink coffee?"

"A *living* ghost," Cody said, with a touch of impatience.

Albert whistled under his breath. "Living or dead, either way, that's *the* whitest white man I ever did see."

"I b-bet," ventured Emmett, "he's one of them,

what-are-they, albiners. Remember the r-rabbit that fella brought through town last year? Kept it in a wicker cage? All white, but for its eyes?"

"I remember!" Mina said. "Pink, they were. Like pink beads of glass."

"There are, by our home, many chipmunks," Saleel said. "They come for the flax-seeds. Once, one was white. But a hawk got it. It couldn't hide."

The Truther-boys, though still clearly scandalized—if perhaps a touch envious of her bravery as well—didn't bother with their gesticulations of protest this time. They, like the others, kept watching as the *Living Ghost* made his way to a table set up near one of the wagons and sat by the shawl-wearing old lady, whose knitting was coming along at a nice pace.

The two conversed briefly, then something happened that sent chills skittering the length of Emmett's spine—the *Living Ghost* turned as if to look in their very direction.

"Down!" Cody dropped into the grass. "Mina, the lamp!"

She snapped closed its folding brass shutters, eliminating the light. Everyone else had followed Cody's example, flattening themselves low to the ground.

"D-did he see us?" Emmett asked.

"Dunno," Cody said.

Saleel tapped his arm. "Mother Sybil?"

"Huh?"

"The old woman. The All-Knowing, from the paper."

"Hey, yeah! So, she's like a . . . a . . . fortune teller."

"A seer," said Saleel, at the same time as Albert said, "A witch."

"You mean she knows we're here?" Mina started to rise for a peek, and Cody stopped her.

"Albert, you look," he said.

"Why me?"

"Like the chipmunk she told us about, only other way 'round. They'll have a harder time seeing you."

Albert's mouth twisted as if he'd bit a sour berry, but he lifted his head cautiously while the others huddled low, hardly daring to breathe.

"He's just drinking his coffee," Albert reported after a moment. "She's still at her knitting. Washing's done, fires mostly being banked down for the night. Looks like they all might be getting ready to turn in, soon. I think we're in the clear."

"Whew." Cody made a big show of arming sweat from his brow. "Are they postin' watches, can you tell?"

"Couple of the men might be fixing to stay up, stools and guns, probably take it in turns. A fella out by the horses, unrolling a bedroll as if he means to sleep there. That's about it."

"The dog?" Cody asked.

"Girl took it with her into one of the wagons."

"All right, then!" Cody grinned around at the rest of them. "We just need to wait a while, let them settle in and go to sleep."

"And what?" Emmett asked, though the sinking in his bellyguts already knew. "They almost s-saw us already; you want to g-go *closer*?"

"Well, sure. Came all this way, I'd like to see more."

Mina, Saleel, and the buck-toothed Truther-boy

bobbed their heads. Albert hesitated, askance, but shrugged. The freckled Truther-boy exchanged an anxious, dismayed glance with Emmett.

"When should we have such another chance?" Saleel spread her hands. "We are not to be allowed to go, otherwise."

"Us, too," Mina said. "Come on, Emmett Pryce, don't you be yella."

"I am not yella!" He did wish his voice hadn't gone squeaky again, but at least he hadn't stuttered, and reckoned that was something.

Freckles, similarly stung in his pride, made a fist and thumped it in the center of his grey-clad chest as if to indicate he wasn't yella neither. Buck-Tooth clapped him approvingly on the shoulder.

"And we did come all this way," Albert said to Emmett.

He heaved a sigh. "Fine. In for a dime, in for a dollar."

"Good man!" Cody dug into his pockets, under his stash of pebbles, and came out with a packet of sassafras candies. He passed them around. At first, the Truthers didn't seem sure what to make of them, but soon enough the sweets made a favorable impression.

While they waited, Albert opened his satchel with the corn biscuits and dried apples. Saleel withdrew from her pursebag some flat, round wafer-crackers made from flax-seed and honey—which proved crispy and crunchy and quite tasty, if they did get stuck in the teeth something fierce—and a lump of soft, sweetish cheese. Freckles had a nearly-full waterskin to supplement Albert's canteen, so they had themselves a nice little meal-break gathered in the rustling grass.

The harmonica and banjo-or-guitar music had long since stopped, the rest of the carnival folk soon retiring to their wagons or tents. For a brief time, hints of candles or lamp-light filtered through cracks, extinguishing one by one.

In the campground, flames dwindled to banked embers, except for where the two men sat sentry with guns at their sides but their postures easy and unconcerned. Every now and again, one would get up and walk around, toss another few sticks on the fire, perhaps stroll a ways off for a piss.

A third man, bedded down by the horses, snored so loud the seven of them could hear him from here. The horses themselves made the infrequent whuffle or snort. But for those sounds, and the rush of wind and feathers as a bird swept by overhead, the night remained quiet.

Emmett was just starting to feel a drowsiness creeping in, was just starting to think fondly of his bed—and then, dolefully, of the long walk back still in store, whenever this adventure might be over—when Cody interrupted Mina's incessant chatter again.

She'd been going gangbusters, keeping her voice down but nonetheless rapid-fire as any trick-shot gunslinger, peppering Saleel with questions. To her credit, the Truther-girl had done a fair job keeping up, even while still getting the shocked, reproving looks from her companions.

No, in fact, they didn't eat meat, unless'n fish counted. Fish, or wild bird's eggs. They did keep some sheep for wool, which also gained them milk to make butter and cheese, but didn't butcher them for meat. What happened when a sheep died some other way, then? Why, it'd be wrapped and buried, same as anyone else.

Seemed wasteful to Emmett, not to mention peculiar. But, these *were* Truthers after all, so who was he to know?

And as for the womenfolk, having more'n one husband? How did that—

"Mina, quit it now," Cody said. He'd tried twice before and she'd shushed him both times with the reminder that their ma surely would want her to ask, might even put it into the eventual Silver River newspaper!

Which also didn't quite make sense to Emmett, given the supposed secrecy of them even being here; what was the good of sneaking out, risking those whippings, if Mina was just to turn right around and tell the whole thing to their ma?

"I'm just—"

"You're just gabbin' her ears off, and b'sides, it looks as quiet over there as is apt to get." He got to his feet, brushing dirt from the seat of his pants. "C'mon."

Emmett's drowsiness fell away, replaced by trepidation, but he followed suit along with the others, and they made their way closer. One of the men on watch was whittling; his partner was nose-deep in a book. Neither stirred as seven small shadows slipped into the mostly-slumbering camp.

From one of the wagons came the sounds of slow creaking and low moans. Cody stifled a smirk. Emmett blushed. From another came snoring much lighter than that of the man bedded down by the horses. A faint light, perhaps of a single candle, flickered through the propped-ajar window shutter of a third.

The colorful paint-jobs and decorations were far more evident up close. Poles held tall canvas flag-banners, depicting some of the acts. Upon one was a huge, hulking figure lifting a locomotive engine over his head—the *Man-Mountain*! Another showed a blindfolded man in sombrero and serape, six-guns gripped in each fist—the *Blind Bandito*! Here, lissome and sleek in a swords-dueling pose, a poster image of the *Deadly Lotus*! And here, arms raised to a host of dark birds, a young girl in fringed and beaded Indian garb—*Princess Crow-Feather*!

"Hey, that's the same girl we saw before," whispered Albert. "The one that was playing with the dog."

Cody acknowledged him with a nod, but his attention was riveted elsewhere. He made as silent a bee-line as he could toward something that looked less like a wagon than like an army-fort on wheels. Sturdy, reinforced, and windowless, it featured a door at each end with fold-down stairs leading to. Above the nearest door, in tall letters, arched the words: *Gallery of Grotesqueries*, with smaller signs reading *Ten Sights For Ten Cents* and *Enter If You Dare!*

On each of the wagon's longer sides were suggestions of monstrous illustrations and garish slash-written scrawls in bile-yellow, blood-red, swamp-green, and dead-black: *Mistakes of Nature! Terrors from the Deep! Night-Stalking Horrors! Inhuman Abominations!*

and so on.

Hanging from the door-latch was a padlock roughly the size of Texas, and Cody scuffed the ground in disgust with his toe. "Nuts," he muttered. "Locked up tighter'n a nun's knickers."

"How 'bout over there?" Albert pointed to a nearby large tent, its flaps tied back to reveal what appeared to be rows of curtained-off shallow pony-stalls facing each other across a floor of strewn straw. Beside the opening, propped on a stand, a sign proclaimed: *Free Bonus Attraction: Exhibits of the Exotic!*

"What's in there?" whispered Mina, crowding Cody's elbow.

"Let's find out!" He glanced around for confirmation. "Yeah?"

"Yeah," said Albert.

"Yes," said Saleel, as Buck-Tooth vigorously nodded.

Freckles and Emmett exchanged their own glance, that accusation of 'yella' still smarting like a smack from a schoolmarm's ruler. They both also nodded, if rather less vigorously.

It did mean going into more of the firelight, but the reading man's back was to them and the whittler had gone for another piss, so they scurried quick across the open space and into the tent. Aside from the faint crunch of straw beneath their footsteps—it was fairly fresh, not still green but not yet dry and rustly—the tent's interior was still and silent and pitch-black. Nothing moved, nothing breathed, but for the seven of them.

"Can't see for tryin'," Mina said. "Should I peep a

crack in the lantern?"

"Best not," Cody said. "Don't want them to notice. Give your eyes a bit."

With what glow as did trickle in, soon enough their eyes did adjust. There were six of the curtained stalls in all, three to a side with a path down the middle. The stalls themselves were plain knock-together planks, the curtains nothing but simple hung blankets. No signs or anything were posted to indicate what might be behind them, and Emmett felt another uneasy squirm wriggle up his spine.

Cody glanced around one more time, then drew a deep breath and took hold of a curtain-edge. "Here goes nothin'."

He whisked it aside and all seven—yes, seven; including both Truther-boys—of them screamed.

3

Mad Skedaddle

TEETH!

An immense jagged maw of them, sharp as knives, sharp as razors! Gaping full half the height of Emmett's pa, wide enough to bite a grown man in half!

Seven voices screaming in unison, and, shameful-though-true, more than two of them sounded like girls. In the moment, though, it didn't much matter, as they were too busy scrambling backward, slipping in straw, tripping over each other, falling down. Emmett had a brief but terrible notion of Mina dropping her lantern and the whole place going up like kindling, but she somehow had presence of mind to hold it high even as she landed hard on her backside with an 'oof!' that cut off her scream.

Then they were up again, all seven, up and running, bolting from the tent like wild mustangs in a thunderstorm. How they managed not to scatter to the four winds, Emmett had no idea, but they stuck together. Again, like mustangs, in a panic-struck herd.

The man who'd been reading by the fire jumped up so fast he knocked his stool over. A ruckus of voices, startled from sleep, rose from the wagons— quite a lot of *what-the-hells* and such. The little dog commenced yipping and yapping a fervor.

They'd be caught, there'd be the very devil to pay; a whipping from his pa was all at once the least of Emmett's worries. A whipping from his pa would be as welcome as a hug, compared to what these fiends might do!

Those *teeth*! Lordy-God-Baby-Jesus he didn't even want to see the rest of what they belonged to! Forget bear-traps and bobcats and Old Man Starkey's tusk-boar-muzzled hounds! The critter behind those ivory blades would make short work of a full-grown ox!

He didn't know where he was going. Nor did he much care. He and Freckles had the lead, Buck-Tooth and Albert hot on their heels, with Saleel and Mina hot on theirs. Cody brought up the rear, playing drover, playing cowboy, urging them to gee-yup, go, go, go, move their feet, gosh-damn-it!

Wagon doors banged open. Lamp and candle-light spilled out. From the corner of his eye, Emmett caught a glimpse of a squat, gnomish stump of a person, with lopsided limbs and an oversized head— "No free shows, y'townie cow-splats!" came a booming bellow surprisingly deep and loud as a cannon volley. **Tom Short, the World's Smallest Negro,** it had to be, shaking a fist at them!

In another wagon doorway, the shawl-wearing old lady who'd been knitting by the fire stood silhouetted, back hunched, hair hanging in crone-straggles . . . and laughing . . . *laughing*, a right witch's cackle, lifting one wizened hand as if to fork a hex-sign. Was the *All-Knowing Mother Sybil* cursing them?

Cringing as he ran, expecting at any instant to hear the crack of the *Blind Bandito's* guns or feel the icy slice of the *Deadly Lotus'* blades, expecting to plow headlong into the immovable mass of *Man-Mountain* or have *Princess Crow-Feather's* fatal flock dive at them all beaks and talons, or the *Living Ghost* manifest before them out of nowhere in a billow of red robes and *Pallid Countenance*, Emmett wished like the dickens he'd never agreed to Cody's hare-brained notion!

They were going to die, all seven of them! Die, or worse! And no one would ever know! To their parents, to everybody in Silver River, they'd just have up and vanished! Gone! Another Lost Meadow mystery, same as those long-ago homesteaders! If anybody even tracked them this far.

But . . . they didn't die. Or worse. No guns, no blades, no beaks and talons, no red-robe billow, nothing. Only a mad, trampling dash through the high grass, flailing at it, stumbling, panting for breath, until finally they couldn't hardly run anymore and staggered to a wheezing halt. Seven in a circle, bent double, sucking air in raggedy, shuddering gasps.

"What'd . . . what'd you all scream for?" puffed Cody, hands planted on his knees.

"Oh, like you din't, too!" Albert kicked a dirt clod at him.

"Only because everyone else did! Gave me a heck of a jump!"

"Horsepucky," said Mina. "You screamed same

time as us."

Emmett, Freckles, and Buck-Tooth indicated agreement.

"Fine, fine, so's maybe I did." Cody gazed back the way they had come. "Nobody on our trail yet, but best we keep movin'. I've had me enough scares for one night."

This met no dispute, and they made for the woodlot at a brisk no-lollygaggers pace, taking occasional shoulder-looks as they went.

"What was it?" Saleel asked, once they'd gotten within the treeline's scant cover. "With the teeth?"

"Dunno," said Albert. "Don't want to, neither."

"B-big, whatever it was," Emmett said. "Never seen the like."

"I think," said Cody, somewhat abashed, "it weren't nothin' but jawbones. Mounted on display like you might do with a wolf's skull, only, there was no skull. Just the jawbones. And the teeth."

"Teeth of *what*, though?" Mina wrapped her arms around herself and shivered. "What's got teeth and jawbones like *that*?"

"Dunno," Albert repeated. "Don't want to, neither."

"We screamed and ran from dead bones?" Saleel arched her eyebrows.

"Big, toothy, scary ones," Mina said.

"Hold up, we only screamed over the dead bones," Cody said. "We ran on account of how the whole camp heard us screamin'."

"Whole *valley* probably heard us screaming," added Albert. "And they set out after us. They would've torn us to bits."

"Or w-worse," Emmett said. "We escaped lucky.

Something wrong with those carnival folk. D-did you *see* the witch hexing on us?"

"You don't think she's a *real* witch . . . " Mina trailed off and bit her lip.

"She knew we were there the whole t-time. Told the ghost, too. I b-bet they *are* up to no good. Wicked. M-maybe evil. Like P-Preacher G-Gaines said."

Another flurry of uneasy looks peered toward Lost Meadow, but a flicker of distant firelight was all there was to be seen.

"Hey, now—" began Cody.

"Think on it," Albert said, as serious as if in school. "That thing we saw, with the teeth, whatever it was? That's part of what they lets you see for *free*. 'Magine what might've been in that fortress-wagon! 'Magine what they might *really* do at their shows! My granpappy's done told me plenty stories about murderers, human sacrifice, cannibals, raisin' the dead—"

"What's cannibals?" asked Mina.

"When you eat people, like that homesteader ma did with her kids," Cody explained.

She stared at him. "Do they . . . well . . . *cook* 'em, like?"

"That homesteader ma prob'ly did."

The Truther-boys, expressions knotted with worry, were having some sort of silent conversation with Saleel, before she turned to the others. "Will they follow us?"

"Might," Albert said. "Cody's right. Best we keep movin'."

Keep moving, they did, though without benefit of lantern or matches this time. The full moon peeked now and then through the trees, painting the western hills a pale sheen. Somewhere up in there was nestled Highwell where the Truthers lived, quite a ways further than just from Silver River. Saleel and the boys had a long walk to get themselves back home. Emmett reckoned he oughtn't fuss too much about being tired, all considered.

"Gosh-sakes, it's quiet," Mina said, after another while of picking their way through the underbrush. "Not so much as a cricket. Was it this quiet before?"

"Well, it ain't quiet now, with you talkin'," Cody said, part in big-brotherly teasing, but part also in irritation.

Albert and Saleel both hissed, "Shh!" at the same time, stopping short, listening intently. Everyone else did the same, and to Emmett it seemed his own pulse pounded audibly, his own breath gusting loud.

Freckles touched Saleel's arm, gesturing some more. She nodded ever-so-slow-like, and whispered soft as a cat's paw, "Someone is out there."

"Let's not let our nerves get our better," Cody said.

Mina shook her head. "No. Someone is. I can feel it."

"I f-feel it, too," whispered Emmett, his mouth gone dust-dry and goosepimples prickling his arms.

He did. It wasn't nerves, no matter what Cody might say. They weren't alone in the woodlot. And it wasn't no owl or night-possum, neither. It was larger. Smarter. *Mean.*

"We's bein' watched." Albert eased his head around, scanning the darkness. "Something *is* out there."

Cody shot him a look as if about to ask why he'd

had to go and say some*thing*, 'stead of some*one*, but before he could, a twig snapped nearby, light and sharp like a derringer—*crack*!

They'd grouped together in a clustered protective clump, shoulder to shoulder, trying to see every whichway at once. Trouble being, they barely *could* see more than a yard or so, and even then little more than ferny bushes, fallen branches, and spindly tree-trunks in the dark.

Oh, but they could *feel*, though. Emmett surely could, and knew the others felt the same. Something big. Something near. Something mean.

"Mina, stay behind me." Cody had given up on suggesting it was nerves, and gone so far as to ready Deadeye with a smooth pebble snugged in the slingshot's leather cup. For once, she obeyed without a hint of sassback, huddling against him like a skittish filly.

Albert gripped the sturdy bough he'd found earlier, treating it much more like a cudgel than a walking-stick now. Buck-Tooth and Freckles each hunkered to pick up rocks from the ground. Saleel dipped a hand into her purse-bag and brought out what might've been an Indian arrowhead affixed to a piece of antler.

Emmett groped through his pockets for anything useful as a weapon, but not finding much. A few loose marbles, his wooden whistle, the kerchief his ma made him carry . . . drat it . . . and was about to stoop for a good throwing-rock or chunk of wood for himself when there was a sudden crunch and crackle from a different direction than the twig-snap had come. But then, *more* twigs snapped back *that* way, and a heavy presence shifted in the shadows. Surrounded?

"Stay close," Cody murmured. However brave he might be trying to sound, a distinct quaver had crept into his tone.

Mina stifled a whimper. Freckles took frantic little sips of air. Albert gulped. Buck-Tooth, beside Emmett, was shaking so much it was a wonder his teeth didn't chatter. Saleel held the arrowhead-tipped antler like a dagger, fist clenched.

A chuffing, ominous grunt reached their ears. Low and guttural. Anticipatory.

What if they'd been right the first time, Cody wrong? The jaws full of jagged-knife teeth not belonging to some dead display thing after all, but an enormous beast very much alive and hungry?

What if the carnival-folk had sent *Man-Mountain* after them, and he truly was an inhuman creature strong enough to pop their heads from their necks with a single squeeze?

What if Old Man Starkey's horrible dogs went silent on the hunt, rather than howling and baying? What if a wolf-pack, or grizzly, or—

A sinister chuckle drifted to them from another direction, curling and coiling, a rattlesnake of cold menace and mirth. From somewhere over past Cody and Mina, Emmett guessed with the only part of his mind still capable of thinking clearly.

But the heavy presence was nearer to where he and Buck-Tooth stood, shifting again as if with deliberate purpose. Maybe wanting them to run. Maybe wanting to give chase.

And from yet a third direction, just ahead of

Albert, there was a sly kind of rustle and groaning creak, what might be made by the protesting leafy limbs of a tree at being climbed by an unwelcome intruder.

Surrounded? he'd wondered. Well, he wondered no more. Surrounded. By who or by what? And did it really matter, when malevolent intentions seemed blatant as could be?

The sinister rattlesnake chuckle—*heh-heh-heh-heh*—sounded again, its curling menace cut short by a rapid succession of *twang-whish-thunk!* as Cody let loose with Deadeye.

Found his mark, too. A howl of surprised rage-pain came next . . . though by then, Cody had already hollered, "Run!" and was doing so, hauling Mina by the hand as he crashed through bushes and low-hanging foliage.

Run, and oh yes, they ran! Plunging after Cody in another wild-mustang stampede, never minding stiff-scraping branches or snagging thorns, never minding foot-tangling roots humping up unseen. They ran with angry death in pursuit, the very ground shuddering at its thunderous footfalls.

Mina yelped, briefly caught by some brambles. Emmett tripped on a log and almost went sprawling, managing not to fall but whacking his knee so hard he wanted to cry. Freckles slammed headlong into a tree, banging his noggin a good 'un; he reeled back in a stagger, but Saleel and Albert caught his arms, practically dragging him. Buck-Tooth charged ahead, passing Cody, who'd spun with another pebble snugged into Deadeye's cup, ready to fire at anything moving behind them. He took a stance over Mina as she fought the rest of the way free, her skin scratched and bleeding, scraps of her clothes caught on thorny hooks.

Though limping near to a hobble and trying not to yowl every step, Emmett paused to help her. His foot bumped a hard, metallic object—the lantern, not just shuttered but extinguished, kerosene sloshing in its hollow guts and leaking in dribbling trickles. If it *had* been still lit . . . but that sparked him a notion.

"Albert! M-matches!" he called.

"What?" But Albert, with Freckles and Saleel, was already gone by.

"I have two left!" Mina held them up, the long household-kind like his own ma used. She struck one on a rough stone. With a sizzle and sulfur-whiff, it flared alight, and after being so long in the darkness, just that lone flame was daybreak.

And if the lone flame was daybreak, the lantern itself was the summer sun. He'd flipped open all the brass shutters before touching fire to wick. It caught immediately, fuel hissing, white-hot-blazing. Noonday-bright shone harsh around them, casting stark-edged shadows to leap and jitter.

Emmett had the briefest impression of a looming, lunging, shaggy-hair mass, some nightmare bear-buffalo *thing* coming at them, not slowing even as Cody let fly another pebble with Deadeye, and he lobbed the lantern at it with every bit of his strength.

The leaks, of course, the dribbling-trickling spills, had also caught immediately. What flew at the beast was an incandescent fireball trailing ribbons of liquid fire.

Although never much of a ball-player, and certainly no sure-shot like Cody, this once when it counted was when Emmett's aim proved true. The fiery missile struck dead-center, splashing burning kerosene, igniting that hairy-woolly-shaggy hide in a genuine conflagration.

Oh, and the shrieks the thing made were unlike any Emmett had ever heard in his life, awful rising catamount cries mixed with the metallic screech of train-wheels when the engineer laid in hard on the brakes, while somehow terribly human too. He saw it go into a flailing, agonized, lurching kind of dance, but then Mina was yanking at him, Cody shouting at him to *go, move, move, go!* So he did, he went, moved, moved, went, leaving that thrashing bonfire to burn.

They caught up with Albert, Saleel, and the Truther-boys at the northern edge of where the woodlot gave way to more open country again.

"Thisaway!" Albert said, waving.

"Are you out of your skull?" Cody replied. "Pigwaller Gulch is thataway!"

"Yeah but Starkey's place is thisaway!"

"*Are* you out of your skull?"

"It's closer! He's got dogs, and guns!"

"Which he'll use on *us*, like as not!"

"We ain't got much choice," Albert said. "I know he's a hateful ol' man and all, but these are some mite bigger problems, don't'cha think? He couldn't be too mad at us for seekin' help!"

"He could be mad at us for Emmett settin' fire to his woodlot!" Cody jerked a thumb over his shoulder at the small-but-strengthening orange glow. With an admiring glance at Emmett, he added, "Hell of a throw, by the way! Gol-damn! *Hell* of a throw!"

"If that is so," said Saleel, supporting the half-dazed Freckles, "we must warn this Starkey before the fire spreads."

"What about town?" asked Mina. "Our folks're there!"

Buck Tooth motioned urgently at Saleel. "And whatever else was hunting us in the woods," she translated for him. "What about those? They might still be after us."

"Dogs . . . and . . . guns." Albert emphasized each word with a jab of his fingers toward the house, visible from here only as the straight-line dark blots of roof and chimney against the starry horizon. "Plus, he's got a mule, and a cart. We can get to town, to our folks, Doc Muldoon—"

Not that his argument needed further emphasis, right then such a furious wail arose from the depths of the woodlot as to make everyone whirl with hearts in their throats.

"That is loss," said Saleel. "Anguish, and revenge."

"How d'you know that?" Mina asked.

"I hear the Truth in it."

"Yeah." Cody looked again at Emmett, this time more grim. "Reckon you just killed somethin's kin, or near-an'-dear."

"I . . . " Emmett faltered, unable to think what to say. He'd never personally killed anything larger than a spider, and only then because one had startled his ma and his pa hadn't been home.

"Later." Albert administered some pushes to get them all going before whatever had bayed its fury from the woodlot came looking for blood.

Emmett kept checking over his shoulder, as much for fire-glow as for pursuit. The former, he noticed, was dimming rather than brightening, which sent a wash of relief through him. He'd be in trouble enough for this night's adventure without becoming known as the boy what burned down Silver River. The latter, he saw none . . . no maddened, menacing shapes loping after them . . . not yet, anyways.

"Hope you know what you're talkin' 'bout," Cody said to Albert. "We get shot, it's on your head."

Albert didn't bother answering except by way of a rude face.

It did seem wrong and foolish, crossing onto Old Man Starkey's land, making directly for the ramshackle house they'd been instructed to steer clear of long as Emmett could remember. The nearer they got, the more ramshackle it looked. So did most of the outbuildings—barn, shed, outhouse, small-smaller-smallest. Only one structure appeared in decent repair, and that was the long, low dog kennel with its fenced yard.

"Quiet here, too," Mina said. "Why's it so quiet?"

"Dogs must be sleepin'," Cody said. "Fine by me. Be anything *but* quiet, otherwise."

"Shush the both of you." Albert nervously approached the porch. Its weathered boards and sagging steps had, like the rest of the place, sure seen better days.

Not so much as a candle now shone through any of the windows. Only a few even had glass panes, and those grime-dulled. Plain tacked-up burlap served instead of curtains.

"Do we knock, or call out, or what?" asked Mina, shifting in an uneasy fidget from foot to foot.

Buck-Tooth huffed a loud breath, closest he'd

come yet to speaking, and pointed back the way they had come. The moonlight touched upon several hunched-over shapes, fanned out like a hunt-pack or searching-party, moving slowly but inexorably in their direction

"We must hide!" said Saleel.

"Damnation!" Cody swore, and bounded up the steps.

The others followed, rough wood creaking under their weight as they jostled for space on the narrow porch. A cane-seated chair and plank table already occupied most of it, the table scarred from cigarette burns, a bottle tipped empty atop it.

"Lordy, don't it stink!" Mina pinched shut her nose.

Stink, it sure did, a dog-stink of piss and shit everywhere, a pig-butchered slaughterhouse stink, and a sour old-man stink of smoke and sweat, stale whiskey and staler beans.

"Mr. Starkey?" Albert's voice quavered. "Sorry to intrude, it's Albert from the liv—"

"Ain't no time for niceties!" Cody went to bang a fist on the door but found it already ajar, so it swung open and he blundered right on into Old Man Starkey's house, with a racket of footsteps, a slip, a curse, and a thudding fall.

Emmett winced, ready for a gruff just-wakened voice to start cussing or the dogs to commence baying to raise hell. The girls rushed to help Cody. Then *they* slipped and fell, with wet-sounding smacks, and Mina screamed, and just like that everyone was in a wild panic again.

The stink in here was far worse, a genuine stench

of blood and offal, gagging thick and meaty, as if Old Man Starkey had just been in the middle of gutting a hog.

Albert alone kept his wits enough to strike a match, though they might've preferred he hadn't.

Old Man Starkey hadn't been gutting a hog.

He'd *been* gutted like one. Sliced from gullet to groin, laid wide open . . . throat torn so deep his head nearly come off . . . one arm hacked all to a mess of raw meat and bone slivers . . . a great gory hollow dug into his midsection . . . his innards become outtards, strewn in lumps and slick tangles . . . a ladder of ribs glistening through shredded flesh . . . and the blood, lordy-mercy, the *blood*!

So *much* blood! More than Emmett would've guessed a body could hold. A puddle of it, a lake, maroon and syrupy! It seeped between the floorboards, dripped down through knotholes. It had splashed like clumsy paint-spatters across the furniture, all up the walls, even the roofbeams!

All that blood, in which Cody, then the girls, had stepped-slipped-fallen. All that blood, in which each of them now trod; they couldn't *not* tread in it, it was everywhere!

Mina screamed, screamed, screamed. Slapping at herself, at her blood-sodden clothes, trying to wipe it off but only smearing it around. Saleel sat as if stunned, her grey Truther-garb sopping scarlet, her enormous eyes so wide they might burst. Cody had flailed over onto his hands and knees, made to push himself up, slipped again, and bellyflopped with a gruesome splash.

Had it been ice, Emmett could've found it comic,

like when they'd gone skating without skates on Cottonwoods' pond last winter, feet going every whichway, laughing as they struggled for balance. Or mud; when it rained hard and the town's main intersection became a morass so as to suck a man's boots clean off his legs . . . on such days, Emmett liked to watch from his pa's office as people tried to navigate it. He'd seen Preacher Gaines once flip himself ass-over-teakettle, and could hardly get through church that next Sunday without sniggering.

But this wasn't ice. This wasn't mud.

This was *blood*, Old Man Starkey's blood, with them tromping and wallowing around in it!

Albert's match fizzled out and Emmett had never been simultaneously so glad for the darkness and aghast by it. He couldn't see, which was good because he didn't *want* to see . . . but he couldn't *see*, which was bad because . . .

One of the Truther-boys bumped into him. He felt his shoe-sole skid and had time for a ridiculous concern as to how upset his ma would be if'n he came home all a mess, as well as time to chide himself for that ridiculous concern, then down he went.

Not a bellyflopper like Cody, thank the dear baby Jesus for that, but a newborn foal's all-fours spraddle with one leg stuck sideways at a crazy angle, one knee planted firmly and both palms sliding in the cold, tacky wetness—

Cold, it had gone *cold*, and he wasn't sure if that was more or less horrible than it would've been were it still *warm*!

He didn't have time to think about it. A hand hooked into his armpit and yanked him up. Other

marrow to jelly. So loud, so close, inside the very dang house! Floorboards groaned under heavy, pursuing weight. The whole structure shook and shuddered and creaked. Rampaging bulls couldn't have made more of a crashing ruckus.

"There!" Saleel pointed at a flap of burlap hanging over a low square gap in the wall, the dogs' exit to their yard.

They went fast as they could, scuffing through filthy straw, kicking aside dented tin plates crusted with the remains of the dogs' last meals and trying not to step on the remains of the dogs themselves.

The enraged roaring drew closer. It had *words* in it, words so as to make Cody's cussing a Sunday sermon in comparison, vile words and viler threats—*gonna getcha little fucks! skin you alive and string you up by your own 'testines, murder my fuckin' brother willya? reach my claws up your asshole and down your throat and pull you 'part from the inside, set him on fire burned him to fuckin' death, dirty fuckers, I'll eat your tongue your eyeballs your heart!*—interspersed with bestial growls and snarls.

Mina was crying, Cody having to practically carry her. Albert's match went out. He might've been crying too. Emmett caught his sleeve on a bent nail poking from a beam, tore the cloth, gouged his arm. *He* wasn't crying, only on account of being too scared; it was all he could do catch a breath.

Freckles reached the burlap flap and raked it open, revealing the shit-strewn moonlit dog-yard with its sturdy fence. Buck-Tooth, bolting for that glimpse of freedom, plowed between Emmett and Albert so hard they each got knocked sideways, falling over or onto dead dogs. The cool, unyielding feel of the stiffening carcass made Emmett's gorge lurch. He rolled off of it and somehow sat up facing back toward the way they'd come.

Just then, the first hunched, shaggy shape leaped down the packed-dirt ramp into the cramped kennel. It landed in a crouch, looking far too big for the confined space, filling it with a menace even the dogs likely never had.

Its stench was rank and wild, the slaughterhouse stink from above—blood, offal, viscera—mixing with something like rotting meat and something like a polecat's musk . . . and something like fresh smoke and burnt hair . . .

Forget his bone marrow turning to jelly; Emmett's marrow was a thin rill of snowslush coursing in his bones. His bladder had gone hot and full again, but he couldn't've loosed it to save his life because all his boyworks felt cinched up in a knot.

Brother, it had said. This thing's *brother* was what he'd hurled the kerosene lantern at, and lit up in a firedance of death.

Then it lunged.

Claws, it had also said, and Emmett saw them as a dull glint in the darkness. He heard the whickering air-slice as they slashed, felt the hot rush of their passage as he threw himself flat. How close, he didn't want to reckon; parting his hair rather than peeling the scalp from his skull. The curved edge of a tin plate dug into his ribs, so he snatched it from the straw and raised it in front of him as the claws whickered at him again.

There was a horrid rending screech, maybe even

a scatter of sparks, but his makeshift shield saved his bacon with a deflecting impact that about jarred his shoulders from their sockets. The tin plate, cleaved into a ragged cluster of pie-wedge shards, flew from his grasp to bang-clatter off into a corner. He fell flat again, in the straw, tangled with the dead dog he'd recently rolled off of. Its matted hide felt mangy and loathsome against his cheek.

Amid more spates of snarls, Emmett was certain he heard words again—*eat . . . your . . . fuckin' . . . tongue*—as he struggled to escape the dog's stiff-limbed, cold embrace. Anything else was lost as Albert grabbed two more tin plates to commence clanging them together like cymbals, yelling, "Yahh! Yaaah!" as he did so. Cody hollered something that might've been "Duck!" and let loose with Deadeye, but wherever the pebble went, Emmett had no idea. He'd flipped himself over again, crawling over the dog, making for the exit where Freckles still held the burlap flap open and reached a hand to help Saleel with Mina.

Buck-Tooth blew past them all like a high wind, plunging out into the dog-yard with nary a glance back. Emmett saw him dash for the fence, no doubt meaning to squirrel it up-and-over and keep right on going. But, as the Truther-boy neared the sturdy row of boards, he pitched forward, making a 'glurk!' kind of noise. Both his arms flew jittering into the air above his head. Momentum carried him the distance to collide with the fence, and there he stayed, scrabbling weakly at the wood while his legs jerked in spasmodic convulsions.

Another match struck, and this one weren't

Albert's. The hiss-flash of light came from outside, as if held by somebody atop the kennel roof. Then it blazed brighter, a hearty torch-orange. And its glow showed poor Buck-Tooth, pinned in place like a bug in a collector's box. Nailed to the fence with the stripe-feathered end of an arrow jutting from the middle of his back.

"Injuns!" Mina shrieked.

"Leegam!" Saleel shrieked too, what Emmett guessed must've been Buck-Tooth's real name.

The voice that spoke from the kennel roof didn't sound like an Indian. It mostly just sounded annoyed. "The fuck's takin' so long in there? They're just goddamn kids; quit playin' with your fuckin' food!"

The creature inside with them uttered another of its guttural growls, then added clear as any ordinary person, "Fuck you, Dex; these li'l fucks killed Rufus!"

If there'd been more meant to follow, Albert didn't wait to find out. A firm step, a sweep-together of plate-bearing hands, and he clanged a double-wallop to both sides of the thing's head. Beast or person or whatever, it reeled like a stunned steer.

A crazy whole lot happened next, too much for Emmett to keep track of all at once. First, he was joining Albert in recklessly pummeling their attacker, fists and feet in a hailstorm of frantic blows, while Cody hollered for them to get out of the way so's he could have a clear shot. Meanwhile, *more* of the hunched and shaggy polecat-stinking things, two or three at least, jostled in the upper doorway as they fought to force their way into the kennel's cramped confines.

Somewhere, Mina shrieked again, a warning, and

Saleel stopped wailing about Leegam to shout *don't-you-touch-him*, and Freckles cried out as if struggling in pain.

Then, Emmett and Albert were also both screaming, Emmett because of a sudden hot splash-dousing of blood in his face, Albert because that blood-splash had come from vicious claws ripping along the side of his head, shredding an ear into stringy gristle.

Now, in the brighter torchlight, Emmett had a better view than he wanted of the creatures, which went on their hind legs like bears but hunched like apes, their thick pelts dark and wiry-woolly as a buffalo's hide in some places but bushed out with sleek fur like a wolf in others . . . their heads, too, were wolfish, with long upper muzzles from which stuck wicked ivory fangs, but their eyes were empty-dead, staring black holes . . .

Under those wolf-muzzles, though . . .

He couldn't be sure what he was seeing and wasn't sure he'd believe it if he could. Looping his arms around Albert's waist, he scooched himself backward on his backside fast as his pushing heels would allow, snowplowing both of them through the dog-piss filthy straw toward the exit to the yard.

All the while, unable to tear his gaze away from what he wasn't sure he was seeing and wasn't sure he could believe.

They had *other* faces underneath, faces covered with unkempt straggles of wild reddish hair. They had other mouths, foul-breathed mouths contorted in snarls of blunt, stubby, yellowed teeth. Other eyes, not empty-dead black holes but small eyes, mean and glittering.

Ugly faces, cruel faces . . . but startlingly *human-*looking faces for all that . . .

And they *had*, sure-to-God, talked!

"You son of a bitch!" Cody cried. Having cast Deadeye aside to draw his buck-knife, he leaped at the one what'd done Albert's ear and struck a rapid flurry of short, hard, sewing-machine jabs.

The thing—the *man?*—balled a big hairy bearlike clawed paw into a fist and slugged Cody square in the breadbasket. As Cody whoofed and bent double, his foe grappled him by the scruff of the neck and the seat of the pants and, with a bum's rush saloon-keeper's throw, sent him headfirst into the kennel wall. Cody's skull met the boards with a ninepins-strike thud. He dropped in a heap and did not move.

Emmett had continued his graceless backward scramble, bringing himself and Albert out into the yard. There, he saw that the man who'd been on the roof—the man who wasn't an Indian despite the bow and deerskin quiver of stripe-feathered arrows slung across his back—had jumped down from his perch with the torch held high.

He was ordinary enough in appearance, lean and narrow-eyed, several days' unshaven, with longish salt-pepper hair under a battered leather hat. A gunbelt strapped his hips. His boots had seen some hard trails.

With his free hand, he had Freckles by the neck, lifting the little Truther-boy until Freckles' cloth shoes desperately toed the dirt in a gallows two-step. Freckles, choking, tugged feebly at the man's iron grip. Saleel shouted, "Let him go!" as she brandished her antler-arrowhead dagger.

Mina looked wildly at Emmett. "Where's Cody?!" Albert, no longer screaming but heaving mewling whimper-sobs somehow much worse, pressed both hands to his ear, blood making thin waterfalls between his fingers. Pinned to the wall, Buck-Tooth—Leegam—had stopped twitching and just hung there, limp as laundry on a line.

"Put that down, girl, a'fore you hurt yourself," the man with the torch told Saleel.

Freckles gurgled. He had gone a color almost grey as his garments.

"I said let him *go*!" Saleel's voice, no longer honey, rang high and unsteady, her whole body shaking, her knuckles bone-white.

"Down the weapon, and I will."

She did. The man released Freckles, who collapsed coughing and hacking. He crawled toward Saleel, herky-jerky as a crippled spider. The Truther-girl knelt to embrace him, though her gaze was its own dagger, hateful and sharp. The man with the torch, seeing it, only grinned.

"Get on out here, boys," he called. "Seems we got us an interestin' development."

The shaggy brutes squeezed one by one through the exit and into the dog-yard, three of them in all, their leader dragging Cody's motionless form by the ankles. Mina screamed yet again when she saw him, head lolling, arms trailing. She might've rushed over there, but Emmett, leaving one arm curled around to support Albert—he was swaying as if about to faint dead away—caught her by the wrist.

Moonlight and torchlight combined fell full upon

the hunched figures, and revealed they really *were* men . . . men wearing wolves' heads atop their own like hats, their own reddish-bearded faces peering from beneath the toothy upper muzzles . . . men wrapped in huge buffalo-hide coats patchworked with scraps from bearskins, wolf-pelts, and coyote fur . . . men with bear's-paw gloves, the still-attached claws strapped to their fingers . . . men whose brows, cheeks, chins, and chests were streaked with blood, less in the manner of warpaint than simply from their gory business.

"*This* cocky shit," snarled the leader, flinging Cody to sprawl boneless in the dirt, "tried to pincushion me with a buck-knife."

"He dead?"

Mina squeaked in dismay.

"Nah. Not yet. Just clonked his head a good'un, knocked his dumb ass out." He nudged his wolf's head hat, or mask, or whatever it was, higher up so's he could turn a hungry look at Emmett. His hair and beard were coppery as a new penny, with bits of bone tied among their straggling locks. "That there skinny pint-sized motherfucker, *he's* the one I want. He's the one what burned Rufus."

It felt of a sudden like there was a wad of dry muslin lodged in Emmett's throat. He tried to gulp it down to no avail.

"Leegam is dead," Saleel, kneeling with her arms around the huddled, trembling Freckles, sent her cold sharp eye-daggers at the man with the bow. "You shot him with an arrow."

He nodded, shrugged. "Didn't want to add a gunshot; we've been makin' enough of a ruckus already. But, the night's still young." He patted the pistol at his hip.

Freckles hid his face in Saleel's shoulder. She bent her head beside his, murmuring soothing reassurances likely as much meant for herself as for the boy.

"Who are you?" Mina demanded. "What do you want? Why'd you hurt Cody? And Albert? If you ain't Injuns, is you outlaws? Did you kill Mr. Starkey and his dogs?"

"Well, ain't you a little busybody bundle of questions?" He tucked a cigarette into the corner of his mouth, and lit it with the torch. "Seems I'm the one should be askin' what a bunch of damn kids're doin' out here. But, since you inquire, name's Dex. These maniacs, they call themselves the Redwolves. You c'n probly see why."

"Who's playin' with their food now?" The lead Redwolf took an ominous step toward Emmett, who cringed. "You all deal with the rest of 'em as you please, but that skinny motherfucker, he's *mine*. He gon' die slow for what he did to Rufus."

"M-mister, p-please, I d-din't . . . " Lordy, his stammer come on so bad he could hardly get a word out, and it was all he could do not to join Albert in shedding tears. Mina about crushed his fingers, she was squeezing so hard.

"Shame t' kill the girls," another Redwolf said, this one short and stocky-built, with bushy muttonchops the color of a sugar maple's autumn leaves. He licked his lips in a truly horrible leer. "Right away, anyhow. Older one there, quite a tender, tasty-lookin' bite."

Dex hoisted an eyebrow. "Rusty, you know how

the boss-man feels about certain carryin's-on."

"Yeah, but he ain't here. He's clear t'other side of town. What he don't know—"

"What he don't know, he might still find out," Dex finished. "And, while he may turn a blind eye to you all's . . . tendencies . . . he's got *some* rules. Girls their age be worth a lot more unspoilt. Sell 'em for good money to that big-city bordella-fella."

"Leave us 'lone," said Mina. "We'll just go home, we won't tell no one. Cody's hurt. Albert, too. They need Doc Muldoon."

He blew a smoke-plume as he laughed. "Now, sweetheart, you know we can't do that. What would you say to the doctor, anyway? Spin him a yarn? I don't think so. B'sides, your Doc Muldoon, he's apt to have his hands full as it is, if he survives 'til mornin'.'"

"Enough jawin'!" The lead Redwolf took another step, which brought him looming over Emmett as he, Albert, and Mina clustered together on the ground. "That was *my* brother you set fire to, you stutterin' fuck. Burned him alive. Ain't no way for a man to die. No way!"

"N-no, I—"

Whatever else he might've tried to say was lost, swatted clean out of his mind even as the man's massive bear-paw glove backhanded him. Whole world went briefly bright as noonday and cyclone-dizzy. Next he knew, he was on his side in the dirt and dog-shit, lip split, jaw feeling pulverized. Even his own pa hadn't ever struck him a blow like that. The pain was such he forgot to breathe.

"Emmett!" Now it was Albert supporting him, while Mina jumped up bold and wroth.

"I take it back!" she yelled. "We *will* tell! We'll tell

the sheriff, and we'll tell our pa, and if the sheriff don't hang you, our pa will put a bullet in your stupid heads!"

"Mina, no!" Albert said, but too late because she went and kicked the lead Redwolf in the shins.

"Hey!" he blurted, startled-like, hopping backward, while the rest of the men busted out great guffaws of laughter.

"Look out, Rory, li'l wildcat bitch gonna whup your ass!" the third Redwolf whooped. "Forget sellin' her, let's sign her up!"

"Shut your pie-hole—ow! Damn it!"

Dex stepped in and took a fistful of Mina's hair, twisting it until she quit kicking, though she did keep twisting and spitting like an angry kitten. "Ain't you a spitfire?" He shook his head, not un-admiringly. "Ain't you just?"

"Oughtta wring her neck," grumbled Rory, bending to rub his shins. His coat-cloak of furs and buffalo hide may have proved too thick for Cody's buck-knife to do much harm, but his legs, protected only by regular trousers, evidently proved another matter.

"Right." Dex gave Mina a push that sent her plopping back down on her bottom beside Emmett and Albert, each of whom grabbed hold of her before she could jump up again. Not, it seemed, that she was going to; her spirit broke and she started sobbing, rocking back and forth. "Tie up the girls, but don't touch 'em otherwise. Then you can have your fun with the rest."

"Dibs on the dark meat," the third Redwolf said, smirking at Albert. He, the thinnest of the three, sported unruly carrot-top corksprings and more freckles than Freckles, and didn't look much older than Cody.

Albert flinched against Emmett, but Emmett's attention was riveted on Rory, who'd shed his clawed bear-paw gloves and was cracking his knuckles like a panful of popping corn. He seemed to be evaluating Emmett as if deciding which part of him to mutilate first, and how long he could make it last.

"Rudy, I swear, somethin's wrong in your brain," said Rusty. "Ever'one knows white meat's better."

"You just ain't got no sophistication. Wouldn't even *try* the Chinee that one time, would you?"

Dex heaved a sigh. "Make it quick, boys. Even you, Rory. Won't deny you your revenge for Rufus, but we still got places to be." He scanned the sky, frowning. "And there's a weird feelin' in the air tonight. Real weird."

As if to emphasize his remark, a bird cawed overhead, loud and raucous.

"Hell's a crow doin' up this late?" asked Rudy.

"Just an owl," Rusty said. His expression took on a disgruntled sulk as he unspooled a length of rope. "Tie 'em up, unspoilt, don't touch 'em . . . big-city fella better pay *real* well . . . "

"He will," Dex assured him.

"Wasn't no owl," insisted Rudy. "I know an owl when I hear one."

"Nighthawk, then. Who gives a good goddamn?" Rusty tried to pry Saleel and Freckles apart, but they clung tenacious as burrs. "Come on, girlie. Don't make it no more difficult than it's gotta be."

"I'll buy you a damn bird-book," Dex said. "Hurry

it up."

Rudy pulled Freckles away from Saleel, and she threw herself to the ground as if she could burr-cling to that, instead. Rusty stood astraddle her, a foot to either side of her hips, as he reached down to wrestle her arms behind her back.

"As for you, sweetheart," Dex added, looking at Mina, "how about you step on over here with Uncle Dex? This ain't gonna be pretty."

She sobbed harder, crawling to her brother instead, shaking him by the shoulders. "Cody! Cody, wake up now, wake up!" But all Cody did was groan a little, his eyelids fluttering.

"You . . . gotta . . . run for it," whispered Albert as Rory took his own sweet time selecting a short-bladed skinning knife from a folding leather case, testing its blade on the callused pad of his thumb, and licking away a line of blood. "Emmett . . . grab Mina and run like blazes."

"I can't leave you all!"

"Do it. Find help. That big one's gonna—"

Someone screamed, screamed so piercing and shrill it might've dropped a flock of bats dead from the sky.

And this time it wasn't one of them. This time, it was Rusty, because Saleel had found her arrowhead-antler dagger, flipped from her belly to her back between his feet, and driven that razor-sharp point of knapped stone right straight up into his personal business.

"Now!" Albert shoved Emmett towards Mina.

Again, all of a sudden, a whole lot was happening at once. Freckles bit Rudy on the arm, no nip but a full-on, sink-yer-teeth-to-the-gums *bite* like he was tearing into a chicken drumstick. Rudy didn't seem to care for being on the other end of the menu, because he let out a shocked scream of his own. Cody had opened his eyes and was blinking around all baffled, probably seeing double or triple of everything. Saleel *rammed* that arrowhead upwards, really skewering Rusty's giblets, turning his scream into a gelded-hog squeal. Rory whirled with skinning knife in hand but jaw agape down to his collarbones. Dex spat out his cigarette, let fall his torch, and reached for his bow. The bird—crow, owl, nighthawk, whatever it was— cawed its raucous cry again, real loud, real close.

Emmett, though he had no idea how, was doing what Albert had told him, grabbing Mina and running like blazes; where, exactly, he was supposed to run wasn't clear in his mind, since back through the kennel and Old Man Starkey's house was the last thing he wanted to do. *Had* to be a gate somewheres in the dog-yard, didn't there?

There was! He caught a glint of latch and hinges, and made for it. Rory hollered something about *don't-shoot-him-he's-mine* but no sense waiting around to see if Dex obliged or not; his shoulders tensed and the skin of his back drew drum-tight as he tried to brace for an arrow pinning him to the fence just like Buck-Tooth.

Mina, bless and cuss her, was fighting every step of the way, trying to go back for Cody. But, a frantic strength was upon Emmett, never mind his injuries and his scrawniness. He ran with her like a fox from the henhouse with a pullet in its jaws, wrenched open the latch, hauled wide the gate, and kept on going.

Freckles ran after them, Rudy's blood on his teeth

and the murderously-irate Rudy on his tail. Rory, still hollering about how Emmett *gotta pay for what he done to Rufus!*, was also in pursuit. Dex, however, was clearly unswayed by this argument, because a stripe-feathered arrow whizzed inches over Emmett's head.

As for Albert? Cody? Saleel? No way to know. He just ran for all he was worth, aware he was going in entirely the wrong direction from town or the safety of Cottonwoods ranch.

Then his entire left leg exploded into lightning-strike agony. He barely noticed losing hold of Mina, barely noticed falling. His leg! His leg! Was he dead? Was he dying? It hurt so bad! What was wrong with—

An arrow, that's what was wrong with it. Stuck all the way through, the glistening tip protruding from the front of his thigh, the feathered end jutting out behind. He wailed at the sky—dark shapes flitted across his vision, blotting out the stars, and did that mean he was dying? Given that Rory was still bearing down on him, he almost hoped so . . . better to be done with it before the vengeful Redwolf went to work with his knife!

Further back, tall in the moonlight, Dex aimed another shot. This one, Emmett just knew, would take him in the heart or the throat or the eye, and he *would* be dead, and that might not be so bad—

The arrow flew true and it seemed sure enough . . . he wished his ma well, wished her escape from his pa, and a good life, and happiness . . . this was it.

Until something lithe and sleek darted out of nowhere with uncanny speed, and something else flashed like liquid quicksilver, and the sheared-in-two pieces of the arrow spun away into the night.

A woman stood over him. A woman clad in form-fitting black leather and bristling with blades, a slim sword held before her.

The *Deadly Lotus* . . . ?

As his astonished mind tried to comprehend, another figure reared up from the high grass. It towered over the Redwolves, half again as tall and twice as broad as Rory, making Rudy look smaller and scrawnier than Emmett. They'd barely even begun to react when the enormous *Man-Mountain* seized each of them by the head and dashed their skulls together like walnuts.

This was just plain crazy. Emmett felt himself tipping sideways, slipping backwards, seesawing down a long fall into a deep, deep, deep hole.

The last thing he heard was a man swearing in pain and panic . . . the last thing he saw was the dark shapes that had earlier flitted across his vision now descending on Dex in a wingstorm of beaks and talons . . . a flock of black birds, pecking out his eyes, slicing his face to the bone . . . set upon him, no doubt, by *Princess Crow-Feather* . . .

And the last thing he thought, as he fell ever deeper, was to wish his ma might be all right without him.

Part Two:

Nasty By Day Or By Night

1

HORSECOCK

IT LOOKED A nice enough place as such things went, Horsecock thought as he surveyed the property from the treeline, alert for signs of activity or wakefulness.

A stout stone-and-log house stood partway up the western slopes of the wooded mountain foothills. It boasted a corn field, a garden plot, a hen coop, a barn big enough for a couple goats and a pony . . . and a view of the valley spreading out, the river a ribbon through it, the town clustered so peaceful-like with no way of knowing the violence about to ensue . . .

Everything appeared quiet. Tidy, well-kept. Womanly touches here and there, nice curtains, picked flowers, a tinkling windchime made from polished pieces of bottle-glass. He'd spied a great orange tomcat slinking around, but no dogs. No neighbors within earshot. Private. Perfect.

Not too big, not too small. *Jist right,* as he remembered from the storybook his mama had read to him from. The one about the golden-haired girl and the bears. When he'd still been known as Horace Cochran, that had been. When he'd still had him a family, a mama he'd adored, a papa he'd admired above all else in the whole wide world.

Before that night the bad men came and took'd it all away. The night his own papa had been revealed not as the brave hero little Horace had always strived to emulate, but as a low and craven coward. The night Mama had begged, had struggled, had wept her broken tears.

The night he hadn't done nothin' neither, for which he'd never forgiven himself. Sure, he'd been knee-high to a jackrabbit then, four years old, maybe five, but he should've at least *tried*.

In his way, he'd been making up for it ever since. Not that anybody else much understood his way. Even among the rest of Nate Bast's gang, known as the Nasty Bastards for all manner of heinous—and some outright inhuman—acts of depravity and violence, he was the one what drew the most sidelong looks.

Seemed a mite unfair, with the Redwolf boys going around *eating* folks, or Tubber getting his thrills holding babies and old ladies under water 'til they drownt, or Gus and Bertrand playing their elaborate betting games on how long it'd take someone to die after being gutshot or bled out or nailed on a cross the way Unholy Joe said Jesus had been. Still, fair or unfair, there it was.

"Can't believe you's lettin' him ride with us," some had complained to Nate. "What he does? What he's done?"

"I ain't forgotten," Nate had said.

"Your own sister—?"

"I said I ain't forgotten. But, aside from that, me and him got no quarrel."

Aside from that. As if Horsecock hadn't done that sister of Nate's an outright favor! She just hadn't appreciated it at the start. They rarely did, in the heat of the moment and all. Took her a while to come 'round. He didn't blame them, though. It were a lot, so to speak, to take in.

Hc was wcll aware Nate had sent him to the outlying homestead on purpose, same as he'd sent the Redwolf boys off to the eastern side.

"Get it out your systems," he'd told them. "Do what you gotta, then join the rest of us in town to finish the main event. T'other fellas don't wanna see all that."

Yeah. Might interfere with their enjoyment of tub-drowning babies and standing over slow-dying shopkeepers with a pocketwatch. Couldn't have the fun spoilt, could they?

Leastways, it meant Horsecock was able to conduct his business alone, as he preferred. He didn't have to have a minder along, because he weren't going to fall into some deranged cannibalistic blood-frenzy and spend the whole night rolling around in entrails glutting himself sick with no one to prod him back on track. He wasn't no damn animal, for damnsakes.

Despite, that was, part of him being named for one. Deservedly, too, as well-attested rumor had it.

Not that he'd at first realized the extent, as it were, of his difference. Wasn't until his stepmother . . . and then, later, at the orphanage . . . and the rancher's wife at the job he'd worked when he run off from the orphanage . . .

Decent women and seasoned whores alike took one look and either took it a challenge or turned him away. "Ought to charge you by the inch," he'd been told, as well as how *they* should be paying *him.*

Most times, though, it just seemed more trouble than it was worth. He endured the joking, the envy, the snide remarks. Being asked how he found tailors, if he had to have his saddles custom-made. Endured it, but within reason.

Some men just plain didn't appreciate what they had. He considered it his responsibility . . . his duty, if perhaps not sacred obligation . . . to remind them what it meant to be a man. A real man.

Satisfied the occupants of the house were not awake and on alert, he settled his hat more firmly atop his head and left the cover of the treeline. He'd left Blondie—his palomino mare, and were there jokes? were there ever!—further down the trail, amid a copse where she'd have grazing in case his business took awhile.

It sometimes did. Sometimes, they was stubborn. Sometimes, they was tricky and caused trouble. Pistol under the pillow, knife beside the bed, fireplace poker within handy reach. There'd been occasions he'd had to hog-tie them more securely than a heifer at branding time, or administer a thorough beating just to get their full attention. Once, an ungrateful lady-type had tried to brain him with a cast-iron skillet still half-full of cold cornbread; he'd sported a prize-winner of a bruise most of the week.

Matters like this, had to be ready for about anything.

He paused halfway to listen for disturbances from

the direction of the town. Nate wanted them to avoid gunshots if possible until they'd secured a good portion of Silver River. Gunshots of both the giving and receiving variety. So far, there'd been none, no doubt partially attributable to most of the Nasty Bastards being fonder of up-close-personal methods anyway. He heard a few faint and distant cries that might've been human screams or might've been nothing but birdcalls, a faraway dog-bark, and little else but the wind in the trees.

Pulling his neckerchief up to his nose so's it covered the lower half of his face, he approached the house. A burgeoning anticipation stirred his loins. Those womanly touches about the place were a promising sign. Young newlywed couple just starting out? Elderlies in the sunset of their years together? Hardy farmer stock with a passel of kids?

He did hope there weren't kids. Kids always complicated. As did hired hands, extraneous in-laws and relations, lodgers, visitors, and anybody else apt to get in the way. His methods required a certain amount of time, with minimal distractions and interruptions.

Didn't appear to be any dolls, balls, or little toy trains about. He reckoned that was a good sign as he climbed the porch steps, treading to the outside edge to avoid creaking. The door proved latched but not locked—trusting sorts, they were—and easy enough to lift by working his knife blade through the crack.

Moments later, he was in a well-kept main room, lit a dim orange from banked coals in the fireplace. The womanly touches continued here, in the form of neatly folded quilts, needlepoint pillows, glass jars filled with decorative pebbles, a braided rag rug, and the like. Place smelled clean and homey, the hearthsmoke with a hint of pinecone, the scents of good cooking lingering about the woodstove.

Rifle over the mantelpiece. Traditional, but not seen much use. Bible upon the mantelpiece . . . likewise. Horsecock had him some troubles believing in any God who'd let the world go on the way it did, allow those such as him and the rest of the Nasty Bastards to run loose and escape the noose.

From beyond a curtained doorway came the sound of gusty log-saw snoring, over the softer sleep-breaths of more feminine lungs. The snores were plenty loud enough to cover any noises of footfalls upon floorboards. He found a lantern on a round table with its top daintied up by a tatted-lace thing, lit it, shielded the light with a cupped hand, and eased the curtain aside for a look.

Nice big four-poster bed, heaped with more quilts . . . another braided rag rug . . . a chest with a padded cushion-seat . . . chairs by the window . . . a washstand and chamber-cabinet . . . all the comforts. And, in the bed, the lucky couple whose luck might just be about to run out.

The man with the log-saw snore was of just-passing-prime years, hair going grey, thinned and receding from a sun-weathered brow, nose that'd likely been busted a time or two in his youth, jawline beginning to droop more toward jowls. The quilts hid the rest of him but for broad night-shirted shoulders. A large, solid build, Horsecock guessed. Hard won by hard work.

As for the wife . . . oh, the snorer certainly seemed

to have done all right for himself in that regard! More than all right. She was some ten or twelve years his younger, chestnut-brown curls framing a face best described as handsome rather than pretty. Well-complected, full-lipped. Again, the quilts hid the particulars, but hinted at a figure firm and sturdy and pleasingly plump.

Did this snoring man deserve such a fine woman? Did he treat her the way a fine woman ought to be treated? Did he truly appreciate his fortune and her charms?

They so rarely did.

He set the lantern on a shelf, between another of those pebble-filled decorative glass jars and a photograph in an oval-shaped pewter frame. Not a wedding portrait, as he would've expected; it showed a child in ruffly christening regalia . . . eyes shut, tiny face expressionless and slack . . . cradled in a pint-sized casket surrounded by lilies.

Folks sure as could be morbid sometimes. Horsecock felt for them, he sincerely did, for them and their loss . . . but was there any call for keeping a baby's death-picture in the bedroom? He tipped the pewter frame glass-down on the shelf. Closed though the kid's eyes may've been, he didn't need any spectatin'.

The brightness from the unshielded lantern disturbed the woman's slumber so that she shifted and mumbled. Her husband responded with a snuffling grunt. Then both of them jolted awake, befuddled and exclaiming, as Horsecock whipped off their comforting cover of quilts and slammed a succession of hammerblow punches into the husband's head.

Their startled confusion played perfect to his advantage. He had the husband dragged from the bed before the man half knew what was happening. Dragged from the bed, then given several more brutal blows—that long-ago busted nose now busted again, crunched like a chicken bone—and hurled into one of the chairs so hard it almost went over.

The wife sprang bolt upright, gasping.

"You scream, or you run," Horsecock told her, "both of you'll be dead in a blink!"

"Maggie, run!" croaked the husband, spitting blood.

Horsecock slugged him in the mouth so that next time he could spit teeth, too. "Were you not listening just now?"

"Walter!" cried the wife, not a scream but perilous-close.

"Best heed me, missus! Don't you budge!" He wrenched Walter's arms behind his back, behind the chair.

She obliged, ample backside pressed to the headboard, hands pressed flat above her bosom. Oh, and he'd been correct in his estimation . . . she was a plump, buxom, fine-figured woman indeed!

Walter lunged, attempting to throw him off. His estimation on the man's build had also been correct. Large, solid, hard won by hard work. Under other circumstances—such as, a proper fair fight—he'd've been one to contend with.

This being, however, far from a fair fight, in a matter of moments Walter was hog-tied as neat as could be, and bound to the chair for good measure.

Blood, spit, and snot drooled onto his nightshirt. Lips split, nose busted, one eye already looking like a currant sinking into a rising bread-dough as his battered face swelled.

"Walter . . . " She'd moved her hands to cover her mouth instead, further muffling the word to a whimper, but flinched as Horsecock shot her another warning glance.

"You," he said to Walter, "sit tight a minute and don't fuss. I need to deal with your missus."

" . . . so much as touch her you . . . "

He drove his fist into Walter's nightshirted belly and the remnants of Walter's supper spewed up to add to the mess. Shame to waste that good cooking, but oh well, so it was.

"Don't hurt him, please, we have some money, not much but some, you can—"

"Not a word, ma'am. Not a word, not a move." He drew his knife. "Hold still, now, y'hear?"

She squinched her eyes shut. Aside from an all-over trembling—for which she could hardly be faulted—she did hold real still as he rounded to her side of the bed.

Walter strained at his bonds. "Stay away from her! Who the hell are you? What do you want?"

"Ma'am," Horsecock said, ignoring him. "Maggie, is it? Maggie, listen to me . . . I'm gonna tie your wrists to this here bedpost—"

Another whimper escaped her, but she could hardly be faulted for that, neither.

"I'll kill you, you bastard, I'll kill you!" Walter bucked in the chair so hard its legs thumped on the floor.

Horsecock continued to ignore him. "—and I'm

gonna gag you so's you keep nice and quiet whilst I conversate with your husband a bit. You understand me? Nod if'n you do."

Without un-squinching her eyes, she nodded. Her nostrils flared with each quick little breath. The combination of her figure, the thin nightdress, and that all-over trembling made for an impressive sight, he had to admit.

As he bound and gagged her—she smelled like apple blossoms—Walter carried on with his swears and struggles. Would give himself the apoplexy if he didn't simmer down.

Horsecock finished securing the missus. She'd kept up whispering what he supposed were prayers until he got the gag in her mouth. Kept her eyes shut, too. Her knees were jammed together so tight it would've taken a charge of dynamite to part 'em.

"There we go," he said. As a considerate gesture, he even tucked one of the quilts back around her. "Gonna talk to your husband now. See what kind of a man he is."

The kind who really *was* gonna give himself the apoplexy, judging by the look of him. Red as a beet, a vein pulsing in his forehead, damn near foaming at the mouth. Or maybe it was just the mixture of spit and bile. Either way, Walter was far from calm, that much was beyond a doubt.

Swinging the other chair around, Horsecock sat opposite him at a companionable conversatin' distance.

He tugged down his neckerchief and smiled. "Wellnow," he said. "Here we are. Mister . . . ?"

"You'll hang for this, you son of a bitch!"

He let the smile widen into a grin. "That's quite some name. Mind if'n I just call you Walter, then? Easier."

"Go to hell!"

"Walter it is. Me, they call me Horsecock. I imagine you don't want to know why. Anyways, not here t' talk about me. I'm here t' talk about you. And your missus."

He could see Maggie at the edge of his periph'ral, noting that she had slitted one eye open the barest sliver to see what was going on. Walter, meanwhile, also had one eye slitted but that was on account of it being buried in that bruising bread-dough puffiness. The other, burning with frustrated fury, glared at him.

"Your missus," Horsecock said, "is, unquestionably, one fine woman. Yes, sir. One very fine woman. Healthy, beautiful, shapely . . . "

" . . . kill you . . . " Walter sputtered.

" . . . keeps you a nice house, cooks you some damn good meals, warms this here bed a right treat I reckon—"

Walter jerked the chair forward a full two inches at that one, its legs scraping on the floor, bunching up the edge of the braided rag rug. He honestly looked about to pop like a tick, so bloated-up mad he was.

As a subtle reminder of who precisely was in charge, Horsecock biffed him another one in the already abused nose. Walter recoiled, snorting, blowing blood-bubbles.

"Havin' us a pleasant chat, here. Let's not ruin it, shall we?" He drew his knife again, lifted and turned it so the blade shone in the light, and rested it across his knee. "Now. What I want to know, Walter, is why a man like you deserves a woman like that."

Perplexitude creased his brow. "She's . . . my wife!"

"Yes, sir, I know. You provide for her. But, do you 'ppreciate her?"

"What?"

"Do you love her? Care for her? Listen to her and take serious what she got's to say? Put her before anyone and anything else on this entire earth?"

"*What?*" Walter repeated.

"Is she," Horsecock said patiently, "*the* most absolute important thing in your whole life?"

"Why . . . she . . . of course . . . what?"

"Would you fight for her? Kill for her? Die for her? Suffer for her? Give all that you possess to spare her a single grief or discomfort?"

"I . . . don't know what you . . . "

"See, when I was a boy," Horsecock said, picking up the knife and idly digging under his thumbnail with the tip, "my papa, he always told me that a man, a *real* man, put his family before everything else in the world. His wife, his children. Before everything else. Before his money, before his pride, before himself. Before God, even, assumin' you're a believer. He told me that. Over and over. A man, a *real* man, would fight for his family. For his wife. Kill for her, die for her, suffer for her, sacrifice for her, whatever it took. Pain, poverty, humiliation, death. You follow what I'm sayin'?"

Walter gave a hesitant, wary nod. Maggie had both eyes open now, following closely. They usually did, when it got to this point.

"Suppose, now, just suppose," Horsecock went on,

"a man might find himself in a situation where he was called upon to prove that. Suppose some stranger come breakin' into your house in the middle of the night, hell-bent on doin' harm. Suppose he wanted money, or else'n he might hurt your family. Do you give him the money?"

Walter's next nod wasn't hesitant, but immediate, almost desperate. "We have—"

Horsecock angled the knife toward him and raised his eyebrows, and Walter shut up. "Right. Then, suppose this stranger who breaks into your house has his mind on somethin' else? Suppose he has a mind to have a go with your missus? Suppose he says if'n you protest or object, he'll cut your fingers off, one by one?"

Both of them, Walter and Maggie, were trembling and tearful by then.

"What do you do?" asked Horsecock, shrugging. "Do you stand down and do nothing, let him have his way? Throw your own wife to his less-than-tender mercies to save your own hide? Or do you resist? Fight? Get yourself killed, knowing that he'll still have his way after, like as not?"

" . . . don't . . . " Walter shook his head, nigh on to blubbering.

"What if the stranger has a mind to do it right in front of you?" he went on. "Makes you sit there and watch whilst he plows your missus? Says he'll let you both go free if'n you do? Do you tell her to go along with it?"

Damn, but he *did* love seeing them like this. Seeing them squirm and stew in their hot bath of selfish shame. Forcing them to confront their innermost. Got him *all* riled up!

He shifted in the chair, had to reach down and do some adjusting on account of just how riled up he was. Walter's gaze flicked quick toward his lap, and flicked away far quicker. Maggie commenced sobbing through her gag.

"How would that be, Walter? What kind of a man could agree to those kind of terms? What kind of man could sit there and watch as some stranger stripped his wife naked as the day she was born? All the while as she's begging and weeping? Strips her naked, rough-handles her titties, splays her thighs wide open, and fucks her half to death? Right in front of him! Right in front of his very eyes, as he watches!"

Walter shook his head some more, so fast he looked palsied.

"Maybe the stranger ain't alone, neither! Maybe he's brung friends, and they each have themselves a go! Laughin' about it while they do! Laughin', flippin' her over to plow the back forty as well, haulin' out to spray their spunk all over her face, makin' her lick them clean once't they're done!"

" . . . please . . . "

Oh, he was broken now, close on to shattered! Slumped limp in the chair, the spirit run out of him like piss down a leg. Maggie, tethered to that bedpost, shuddered pitifully, just wracked head to toe with sobs.

Horsecock paused, lingering, savoring. Then he leaned forward, bracing his elbows on his knees. "Now, seems to me, a man who would allow something like that ain't such a *real* man at all. No matter how big he talks, no matter what he's said, when it gets right down to it . . . to do that . . . no, ain't no sort of a *real* man, is he?"

" . . . no . . . " said Walter. "No, Not a real man."

"And not a good husband."

"No. Not . . . not a good husband."

"Because a real man, a good husband, will do anything to protect his family, am I right? Endure any amount of pain, suffering, or humiliation to spare his beloved wife that kind of . . . indignity. And he *sure* as hell would have no cause later to blame *her* for it, now, would he? Never mind not being a real man or a good husband, that just plain ain't being a decent human being, is it? That's low even for a *rat*, don't you think?"

Walter nodded.

"Why, and even if she sacrifices herself voluntary—they do that sometimes, you know, sayin' to the stranger, *do what you gotta to me, just don't hurt my husband, don't hurt my family*; they're better'n us in that way, women can be—he might blame her for it all the more. Feel diminished, like. Robbed. Cheated. Betrayed. Unable to look on her again with anything but disgust. As if *she* were at fault, despite it havin' been to spare *him*. See what I mean?"

Again, chin quivering, Walter nodded.

"Ain't fair, is it?"

"No, sir."

"Would a wife be within her rights to hate that husband for it, d'you reckon? For givin' her up that easily, her honor, her person? For treatin' her so, after? Some might argue she would. Hell, some might argue she'd be within her rights to poison him or push him down a well, and good riddance."

To this, also, Walter could not help but indicate his agreement.

"But, that's not so much neither here nor there, is it?" Horsecock waved it aside. "I think we see eye to eye on the subject in general, Walter. Don't you? On what makes a man a real man and all? Yes, I think we do. I'm glad we do. I'm glad as we understand each other."

He hitched his chair a bit closer and Walter tensed up as if wanting to hitch his twice as far back.

"So, what if, let's suppose, the stranger offers up a choice? What if he says the wife'll be left alone, so long as the husband undertakes certain of those . . . indignities . . . in her stead? Some are like that, you know, fellas with more of an eye for other fellas. Back forty's a back forty, after all. Face is a face, and any tongue can lick as clean as the next."

The aghast horror dawning upon Walter's countenance was a treat to behold, as was the choked noises of negation Maggie managed to force through her gag.

Horsecock chuckled, dropping hand to lap again for another hefty adjustment. Trousers had got some bit confining, they had. Wouldn't mind undoing them to let his namesake spring free and stand tall and take the air. Wouldn't mind giving it a few firm strokes, to prime the pump, as it were.

"Think such a prospect might change the calculations, Walter?" he asked. "How would that factor in to the perception of being a real man? Seems a trick question, don't it? A genuine philosophical dilemma, the high-hat professor types might say."

" . . . why are you doing this, why you got to do

this . . . ?" Walter pleaded, and had there ever been a point in all his life up 'til now he looked so utterly wretched?

Horsecock doubted it. They were at the brink, they were. Backed to the very brink and teetering upon it, like boothills on a crumbling canyon's edge.

"Fascinatin' to contemplate, really," he said, casually, almost idly, as he unbuckled his belt. "Learn a lot about a person that way."

Top button.

"Someone you thought you knew."

Second button.

"Someone you maybe even loved."

Third.

"Learn a lot about your own self, far's that goes."

Fourth.

"In such a situation, under such circumstances, what *would* a man do?"

Fifth and final button.

He exhaled with satisfaction as he brought out the implement what had earned him his moniker so long ago—seen him bathing, his stepmother had, the brazen bitch who'd come into their house after Horace's beloved mama drank down a full bottle of tincture of opium; *Lord have mercy, boy!* she'd said, *that's some horse-cock you got on you! Get on over here and I'll show you what t'do with it . . . but don't tell your papa.*

But he, even at his still-youthful age, didn't need her to show him what t'do with it. He already knew. Had already known since that night the bad men had their fun. The night his papa proved nothing but bluff and bluster despite all his big talk.

As for bidding him not tell his papa? Hardly

mattered; hussy'd gone and done that herself. Drunk and angry, hurlin' words like weapons. Oh, and there'd been a fight then, hadn't there? A fight ending up with both of them dead, and Horace on his way to the orphanage, with blood on his hands.

Years gone, that was, though, Years gone, and now he was here, where the sight was not greeted with lustfulness, but abject dread.

"What about you, Walter?" he said. "What'll *you* do?"

2

Easy Money

SOME OF THE OTHERS, sick fucks as they were, just *had* to have them their games to play. Had to have their fun. Had to make their point or deliver their message, such as it may be. As if the violence couldn't simply be quickest means to an end. As if money alone somehow weren't motive or reason enough.

Sick fucks, they were, sick fucks indeed.

It was profit what mattered. Valuables. Preferably of the uncumbersome and readily portable variety. Folding paper or cold hard cash-in-coin. Gems. Jewelry. Precious metals in any form—gold dust, nuggets, silver flatware. The odd pearl-handled pistol here, the odd enamel-lacquer trinket box there.

Livestock, not so much far as Leonard Loke was concerned. He'd done his share of cattle-rustling and horse-thieving, and while there was sound profit to be had on the re-sale, dealing with the animals was one non-stop pain in the nethers.

Land deeds, he found of even less interest. Deed

itself might be portable . . . land itself sure as hell not. Land stayed put. Land anchored a man. He gave nary half a shit for that, thank you kindly.

Ransomages and other such personages also posed far too much hassle for his liking. So many opportunities for things to go awry. Feeding them, transporting them, keeping them hid and meek and mild . . . the chance a prize payoff might up and die before collection, rendering all that previous effort for naught . . . the whims of simple human nature, like the time the captive and a guard had up and fallen in love and run off together; what a fuckarow that had been!

No, give him a good old-fashioned stick-up any day. Give him a bank, a payroll train, a stagecoach to rob.

Or, as case may be, a town to sack.

A town perhaps not such a ripe plum as first promised, though, and for that he shot Pete a dirty look as they left the doctor's house.

"Whaaaat?" Pete whined. "Told you, been years since I been here; used to be a genuine boom-town!"

"From boom to bust, more like," Shotgun Sue said. "Sorriest haul I ever did see."

She led the way long-strided, a bag slung over the shoulder not occupied with toting her beloved Johnny Thunder. The double-barrels rode easy on her leather coat, Johnny having thus far been a quiet partner in the evening's affairs. Quiet, but not idle; blood, hair, and bits of brain clotted the walnut stock. Quite adept at slamming that stock against a man's temple or into his larynx, was Sue. Dropped them about as quick as a full-bore blast of buckshot.

Not that she'd delivered the doctor such a blow.

No, sir, his end had come courtesy of Otto's broad-bladed knife, thrust up between the ribs at a practiced angle. On the rare occasions he didn't skewer the heart on the initial strike, a swift sideways tug usually finished the trick.

Otto, who most times had less to say even than Johnny Thunder, brought up the rear of their quintet, walking apace with Billy-Jack. They, and Sue, shared Leonard's opinions on the subject of easy profit and minimal fussing around. Made them somewhat of a minority stacked up beside the others, the sick fucks, out there this very moment.

"You said there was a bank," Billy-Jack said to Pete.

"Used to be! Right there!"

"That's a schoolhouse, you damn fool."

"A schoolhouse now, yeah! But used to be a bank!"

"So, they didn't have a schoolhouse when you was growing up here?" Sue scoffed. "Explains a fair lot."

"There was! I just . . . wasn't much for schooling!"

"Paint me shocked," Leonard said.

"You ain't pulling a fast one, are ya?" Billy-Jack squinted at Pete. "Filled up our heads with falsehoods?" His voice climbed to imitate Pete's whiny register. "*Silver River fair to brimming with loot, saloons and whorehouses far as the eye can see, rich miners and richer ranchers, folks all soft and complacent-like, won't hardly throw a fuss—*"

"Last part's been right, anyhow," Leonard said.

Which was true enough. Their group had hit two ranches and a miner's claim on their way into town proper, meeting next-to-no resistance. Of course, it helped they were seasoned hands at this—four of the five of them, leastways; just his luck Nate stuck him with Pete, but it was that or Unholy Joe, and Leonard would sooner drink lye than have Unholy Joe at his back. At any rate, they'd so far been successful, if somewhat disappointed by their take.

Otto kept their official tally, but Leonard wasn't of a bad mind for figuring himself and made it fourteen dead already. Fourteen dead, not a shot fired, the rest of the valley none the wiser. Knife-work, mostly, though Billy-Jack specialized in neck-snapping. He was a small sort, but wiry and surprising strong for his size.

At the ranches, they'd gone through the bunkhouses like a plague, barely stirring a sound more than a crack or a gurgle. Men dead in their beds with no idea the end had come. One of the ranchers had awakened, all *who's there I have a gun* into the shadowy bedroom, but Otto'd been on him before anything much could come of it. The rancher's wife, also wakened, tried to flee and ran straight into Billy-Jack's waiting arms. Snap.

The hauls, though, indeed, thus far left something to be desired. They'd grabbed up what there was to be grabbed, consoling themselves with the notion they'd find sweeter pickings as they went along.

"Someone in this shit-hole's got to have money," Billy-Jack said. "Where ought we try next? The church?"

Leonard shook his head. "Joe'll be heading there, and you know how he gets."

"A saloon?" Sue suggested.

"Where they at?"

"Looks like only one left," Pete said. "The Silver

Bell, down by the post office."

She turned to regard him with open contempt. "Anything around here actually still *is* how you spun it?"

"*Whole place just brimming with loot,*" Billy-Jack imitated again. He spat. "Judas fuck. Wasting our damn time."

"Ah, hey," Leonard said. "We're doing all right. Any dollar in your pocket more than what you started with is a day's work well done, remember."

"The mercantile, then," Pete said. "I know me for a goddamn *fact* there's money there."

Otto grunted, and Sue chuffed a laugh. "Yeah, the day's till," she said. "Raking it in, I bet they are. Cornmeal, ten-penny nails, pickle barrel, canned beans—"

"No, there's money. There is." Pete's brow darkened. "Those spinster bitches what run the place, they never trusted for banks even when there was one. Miserly skinflints the both of them. Stuff their mattresses with cash, I shouldn't wonder, or bury it in jars under the root-cellar."

"How the hell would you know?" asked Billy-Jack.

"My aunts, ain't they?"

Leonard pinched the bridge of his nose. "Goddamn it."

"The old man, their pa, was no better," Pete went on. "Blind eye and deaf ear to the needs of his very own only son . . . *my* pa . . . sooner see him beat black-and-blue in the street than lend a hand to help when he landed in a pinch—"

"I got no patience for this," Leonard said. "Save your tragic fuckin' story for someone who cares. You sure they got money?"

"Yeah. He left them a damn fortune, *and* the store. But would they spare even a dime a week's extra allowance for the nephew what they took in? Let him dip into the penny-candy jar now and then? I—"

"I *said*," repeated Leonard, "I got no patience for this. We'll take you at your word for it. But, we go in there and come up dry? Or we go in there and you start making some big dramatic production? I will personally slit your throat and throw you in the river."

"I'll help tote your corpse," said Billy-Jack.

"I'm trying to do a favor, here—"

"Shut your yap, kid, before I shut it for you," Sue said, patting the shotgun's stock. "Johnny Thunder here hasn't knocked out any teeth yet tonight."

Pete shut his yap, wearing a sulky expression that just begged to be smacked off his face.

"We'll head for the mercantile," Leonard said. "Roundabout, though, and on the hush. No one's stirred a ruckus yet; longer we can keep it that way, the better. You heard what Nate said."

They set off, circling behind the wagonwright and a lumberyard. Both seemed as yet undisturbed, and the town for the most part continued its oblivious slumber.

"Only a matter of time until some of those sick fucks let their games run away with them," Sue muttered, falling in at Leonard's elbow. "Then all ruckus breaks loose, wait and see."

"Tell me something I don't know."

"In a way, I suppose, we're doing these folks a kindness," she said.

"Oh, don't now *you* start in on philosophical

musings. We're here for what we're here for. And what are we here for?"

"Profit."

"Damn right."

The mercantile building, when they reached it, did have potential. Miserly skinflints or not, whoever ran it made sure it was in tip-top shape. Its appearance spoke of regular upkeep, diligent care, and efforts made to present an establishment of some means. High ceiling, glass windows, tall shelves laden with an impressive variety of goods. Living quarters above, including an upper balcony with ornately carved railing overlooking the main thoroughfare.

"I might've been wrong about the cornmeal and beans," Sue allowed.

"Likely they stock those as well," Leonard said. "But some cost's gone into it, no mistake."

Billy-Jack returned from a scouting circuit. "Back way looks best," he reported. "No facing neighbors, lower door and exterior stair to an upper. Snug little shed where a watchman sleeps, but Otto did for him already."

"With no fuss?"

"Just a fart." Billy-Jack snickered. "Some doozy of a fart, though. Think Otto would've stabbed him twice for that."

"All right." Leonard cast a listen. He heard the faint strains of bestial howls in the distance—fucking Redwolves—and a splashing from the nearby bathhouse that could've meant nothing more than a late-night scrub but was probably Tubber indulging himself. Sick fuck. Had there been a baby crying earlier? Over to the bakery? Might've been. Not now, though, there wasn't.

As they sidled down the alleyway between mercantile and bathhouse, Shotgun Sue fell in at Leonard's elbow again. "Kid's gonna cause a problem."

"Yeah. I figure. Be ready, huh?"

"Always am." She patted Johnny Thunder.

The back of the building matched Billy-Jack's description, down to the lingering ghost of the watchman's dying fart. That, or a family of skunks who'd gorged on rotten eggs, been set afire, and left to rot in an overflowed privy.

"Cover the downstairs," Leonard told Otto, receiving a curt nod in response. "Rest of you, with me. Up and in, quick and quiet." He glanced wryly at Pete, whose recollection of the exact layout had been anything but exact. Nor was he able to guess how many the live-in household might currently number.

"Used to be," he said, "there was a chef and two maids. A slop boy, too, but they dismissed him when—"

"Let me guess," Sue said. "Had you take over, do his work for free. Penny saved, penny earned, and all that. Make you sleep in the kitchen?"

"In the attic. Turned my pa's old room into a sewing parlor, they did."

"Enough with the Dickensian bullshit," Leonard said. "Let's go."

They went, Otto muscling the lower door to admit himself to the downstairs storefront, Sue busting a windowpane to reach in and unlatch the upper. The tinkle of breaking glass was about the most noise they'd made thus far.

Even so, it did not go unheard; the closest inner door off the hallway creaked open and a young woman emerged, struggling into a robe.

"—that McCall troublemaker with his slingshot again—" she grumbled to someone else still in the room, but got no further before Sue introduced her to Johnny Thunder's walnut stock. The maid dropped loose-jointed as a cut-strings marionette.

"Sarah?" said a second woman yet within, bedclothes rustling as she no doubt sat up. "Did you step on glass? Did you fall?"

Small and wiry Billy-Jack was past Sue and over Sarah in a trice. A cotframe creaked, the bedclothes rustled again, and a startled little cry ended with a brittle snap.

Leonard took the next door, which let onto a room flooded with moonlight. A portly man of middle years occupied the bed, smiling and smacking his lips in his sleep as if dreaming of oysters in cream sauce. One slit throat later, and planning the next day's menu was no longer his concern.

From further along the hall came the sounds of a scuffle. Some piece of furniture went over, a louder cascade of tinkling breakage suggesting fragile items shattering to their doom.

"Mildred!" a woman called. "Mildred, help,— mmf!"

"Die, you damn hag-bat, *die!*"

Pete, of course. Goddamn Pete. As, from another room, there issued an alarmed, "Twyla? What is it? Twyla?!"

"Shit." Leonard left the chef's room at a run,

meeting Sue and Billy-Jack mid-passage. He motioned the two of them one way, whilst he went the other, to see what fuckery of a mess Pete had stirred up.

This room also had wide windows through which moonlight fell, filtered by frilly sheer linen curtains. It smelled almost cloyingly of lavender, rosewater, and toiletry-powder. Knickknacks and trinkets cluttered every surface from hell to breakfast: crystal this, ceramic that, vases, figurines of angels and elegant-gowned ladies and beribboned pussy-cats.

Pete crouched astride the mattress, knees pinning the coverlet taut over a struggling form . . . arms trapped at the sides, legs churning, head buried under a sateen-looking pillowcushion. His shoulders shook from the effort of pressing it down smothering-hard.

"Miserable bitch!" he hollered. "No more'n what you deserve—"

"Wake the world, why don't you, you mule's ass idiot!" hissed Leonard, slugging him in the ear.

A mule's ass idiot move of his own, it turned out, because the punch sent the kid cartwheeling off the bed and into a ridiculously precarious thin-legged table upon which clustered about two dozen more goddamn knickknacks. Just to add gravy to the taters, Pete kept his grip on the pillowcushion, tearing it from the face of the woman he'd been trying to smother.

She, freed from confinement, popped up quicker than a jack-in-the-box. Every bit the white-haired and wizened dowager the décor had led him to expect, she was nonetheless far from fragile or feeble. Already mustering another shout, she snatched a tall, narrow, fluted glass something-or-other from her headboard and let fly. It hit Leonard spang in the forehead and exploded into glittering shards.

Stinging from myriad tiny cuts, needle-slivers poking at his eye, he buried his knife in her chest. It met all the resistance of stabbing into a wicker basket. Silenced mid-shout, she gave him an affronted look—*how rude!*—and sank back with her spidery fingers twitching at the handle.

"The hell?" whispered Sue, harsh, from the doorway.

"The other?" Leonard asked, swiping at his face in hopes of dislodging the glass shards without cutting himself further. Or, God forbid, driving any deeper into his eyes.

"Got her." She hefted Johnny Thunder, a fresh wad of iron-grey hair now blood-glued to the stock.

"Anyone else?"

"Not up here."

"What about him?" Billy-Jack, deftly avoiding the cluttered room's obstacles, had reached Pete, who lay dazed amid the ruins of china shepherdesses, crystal butterflies, and sprigs of dried lavender spilled from broken vases.

"Get his idiot mule's ass up," Leonard snarled. "Sue, check with Otto. See if we raised the whole fucking town with all that."

Pete had the gall and the nerve, once he cleared his head, to keep whining. "You killed her! I wanted to! I owed her one!"

"Shut up."

"What about Aunt Mildred? Did—"

Billy-Jack's arm hooked around Pete's neck. "Man

said shut up."

"Glkk." said Pete.

"Hold him," Leonard said. He went to the top of the stairs, and met Sue as she ascended.

"Think we're good," she said. "Otto's been watching the street. Activity in some of the buildings. Might just be our people."

"Might not."

"Yeah. Might not. But, for now, no alarms."

"All right."

They regrouped below, in the main area of the mercantile. Pete sat sullen, arms crossed, waiting for the dressing-down he knew would be coming. Billy-Jack stayed nearby, while Sue and Otto began going through the till.

Leonard, for his part, found a hand mirror and tweezers, and set about picking pieces of glass from his face. "Lucky I still got both eyes," he said. "Damn, that smarts."

"Tell you one thing, though, should brighten your spirits," Sue said. "Idiot mule's ass wasn't lying about the cash. Full till, *and* a strongbox tucked in under. Made us a killin', and we ain't even checked their mattresses or dug up the root-cellar yet."

"Not t' mention jewelry," Billy-Jack said. "The other one, the tall one what Sue let have it, big ol' jewelry box there on her vanity. Maybe paste, but looked real to me."

"Saw a tea set, pure silver," Sue added.

"Take what you want of the silver and jewelry and stuff," said Pete, "but I reckon most of the cash money ought go to me."

"Oh, do you now?" Leonard asked flatly.

"Well sure. My idea, wasn't it? Coming here. And this . . . " he waved around the store. "All this ought be mine anyways. By rights."

"Damn, kid." Sue sighed. "You got a lot left to learn, don't you?"

"What? Make up for how they treated my pa, and how they treated me. My inheritance, like."

"Your inheritance, like," Leonard echoed.

Sue caught his eye. "Told you."

"Yes, you did."

"It's only fair—"

Otto, busy stuffing fistfuls of money into burlap sacks, snorted.

"Fair," said Billy-Jack. "Well, Jesus wept, how about that?"

"Whaaaat?" whined Pete some more. "You all get the whole rest of the town; this here belongs to me!"

"By fuck, you *are* an idiot," Leonard said. He hiked his chin to Billy-Jack, who snugged the crook of his elbow around the kid's neck again.

"Wait!" croaked Pete.

"Nope." Billy-Jack jerked his arm.

Bone cracked. Pete's heels drummed briefly. A puddle of piss spread around him. He slumped, and when Billy-Jack let go, slid slowly over to lie dead with that sulky, disbelieving pout froze on his visage.

3

Tick-Tock Pocketwatch

"**W**ELL, WELL, WELL,** wouldya lookee here, Bertrand? We caught ourselves a lawman!"

"So we did, Gus old chap! Jolly good, jolly good!"

The voices filtered through a fog of pain, but before he even attempted to open his eyes, Travis went for his gun.

Or, tried to.

He slapped leather and found the holster empty.

Then he recalled—he'd drawn already, drawn as soon as he stepped into Nan's and realized something had gone very wrong in his peaceful little town.

One moment, there he'd been, sleeping like a baby, all well in the world . . . the next, some sound or instinct had brought him to wakefulness. A raised voice? Someone shouting? Breaking glass? Trouble?

Silver River had been no stranger to trouble, back in the day. They'd had their share of miners kicking it up in the saloons, fist-fights over women, street-fights over insults. They'd had thieves and rustlers, and a shot-my-pa revenge killin' or two. Once, an honest-to-God Injun raid. Occasional ugliness over the coloreds, and suspicions of the Truther-folk up Highwell. Nothing out of the ordinary.

Lately, though, lately, it'd been quiet, and that was the way he liked it. Those who said the town was failing, dying . . . those who yearned for the bustling city-plans and railroad and all . . . they could keep their grumblings. Travis was just as happy to get by with only himself and a deputy to keep order.

He'd almost rolled over and gone back to sleep. An argument was all, a smashed whiskey bottle. Nothing that couldn't wait until morning.

Then he'd sighed and sat up. Tempting as it was to ignore whatever had disturbed his fine slumber, he *was* still the sheriff and supposed he did still have a job to do. Mayor Fritt would give him no end of misery if he didn't. So, he'd gotten out of his warm bed, dressed, donned hat and boots and gunbelt, and ventured yawning out into the dark streets of Silver River to see what was what.

Right away, he noticed a lamp lit over at Nan's Cookpot, and that did strike him peculiar. Early to bed and early to rise was Nan's live-by; what could she possibly be doing up at this hour? He headed across, pausing briefly to glance one way toward the saloon—quiescent; no late-drinkers arguing there—and the other toward the general store and the bathhouse. A bothersome niggling struck him, but he couldn't quite lay a finger on it, so continued to the Cookpot.

He knew the place well. Everyone in town did; it was where most of them who didn't have wives or a flair for cooking took their meals twice or thrice a day. Bring your own bowl or mug, or rent one for a nickel extra, and get ladled out a hearty dollop of whatever was on the menu. Mornings, might be oatmeal or rice porridge or boiled fruit. Noontimes, creamed corn, split pea soup, maybe pork-n-beans. Supper, most likely stew or chili, with chicken-n-dumplins on Sundays. All subject to vary, according to what Nan had managed to get her hands on that day. She worked close with the Gillinses from the bakery, so there'd also be toast or cornbread or biscuits available more often than not. And coffee; Nan brewed it by the gallon, dark and bitter and strong enough to punch a hole through a brick wall.

Been a long time, though, since any hungry souls had gone poking around uninvited in search of scraps. Last one that had—some fool desperado of a would-be stagecoach robber on the run from Fort Winston—Nan rang his bell proper with her favorite ladle, then personally brought him over his dinners the whole while he sat in Travis' jail cell waiting on the soldiers to come fetch him.

"Got hisself caught looking for a decent feed," she'd said. "Least I can do is see he gets it; you know they won't give him more'n gruel-water in prison. Gruel-water, and then the noose. Shame for anyone to die on a hollow belly."

That was Nan, right enough. So, when Travis moseyed on into her establishment, where the aromas of that evening's beef-and-lentil yet lingered, he'd expected trouble of a similar nature, nothing worse.

He had *not* expected to see Nan, and Halfwit Charley who helped out at the place, each strapped face-down to one of the long dining-room tables, heads hanging over the edge, wrists bound behind them. A couple of the bins Nan used for collecting up dirty dishes had been set below them like catch-basins. As they squirmed and made muffled noises, he saw they'd both been gagged with tied twists of knotted cloth.

Nor had he expected to see a man, dapper as could be in a sharp suit with starched collar and mother-of-pearl cufflinks, debating over a spread out butcher's selection of hatchets and cleavers. This dandy, whose tipped-back bowler hat revealed an aristocratic face and fastidiously waxed mustache, twirled an ornate pocketwatch by its chain as he pondered the various implements. All of which, Travis knew, would be honed nice and sharp; it was one of Charley's duties, and, halfwit or not, he did it well.

Any vestiges of sleepiness fell away fast. He went for his gun, drew it fast, drew it smooth. "Whoever the hell you are, mister—" was as far as he got before . . .

What?

Before something had happened. Someone had hit him, got the drop on him, struck him from behind. A starburst like Chinese New Year fireworks went off inside his skull. Next he knew, he was on the floor, hearing those voices, fighting through that fog of pain.

Going again for his gun, and finding his holster empty.

Had he dropped it? He must've.

Opening his eyes showed him the well-swept boards—another of Charley's duties, not so much as a crumb left behind to attract mice—and the legs of chairs and benches around the long tables. His badge, which had been in his vest pocket rather than pinned on, glittered its silvery star-shape in the lamplight.

His gun lay some distance beyond that . . . with a scuffed cowboy boot resting casual-like atop its barrel. Gaze tracking upward, he followed a denim-clad leg up to a broad leather bullet-belt, two six-guns, a brass buckle in a ram's head design, and a faded plaid flannel shirt. The man to whom all this belonged was nobody Travis knew—scarred and scruffy, as grimy as his partner was dapper—but he didn't need to know him to know what he meant. Some faces were just plain made for wanted posters. This man's was one of them.

"A lawman," he said again. "How do you like that, Bertrand? How the berry-blue fuck, I ask, do you like that?"

"Much better with him down there and us up here," said the other.

Bertrand. Bertrand, and, if Travis had heard correctly, Gus.

"*Too-shay*, as the Frenchies say. *Too-shay* indeed."

"Most fortunate you were there to intervene. He could have thrown quite a damper on our plans."

"One more reason you keep me around."

"Heaven knows, it isn't for the genteel company or gentlemanly discourse."

Gus guffawed as he bent and picked up Travis' gun. In his free hand, he held a weighted leather bag, a kosh, probably filled with lead shot . . . perfect for administering a clout to the head, as Travis could now testify.

He had to get up. Had to do something. Whatever

mischief these men were up to wasn't good, and all around him the law-abiding citizens of Silver River slept unknowing. Depending on *him* to keep them safe. Wasn't that, as Mayor Fritt reminded him at every opportunity, what they paid him for? Paid them both for, him and J.B., though his damn deputy was probably over at the Bell, basking in post-coital bliss with the lovely Lacy Cavanaugh, right this very moment.

While he, here he was, flat on the floor, feeling like the telegraph lines between his brains and his body had unstrung from their poles. Here he was, with Nan's scared eyes imploring him over the knotted rag in her mouth—a fresh welt at her temple told him she'd also taken a blow, and who could *do* such a thing? To round, kind-faced, matronly *Nan?* Not to mention poor Charley, harmless as they came!

Anger cleared more of the fog and lent him strength to try to rise, but he'd barely begun to move when something pressed hard at the back of his neck.

"Ah-ah-ah, my fine constable," Bertrand said. "Nothing too hasty now, shall we? That's the tip of my cane you feel at your nape. An exquisite piece, this. A collector's item. Ebony, you know, fitted with silver. The knob hides a rather clever little spring-loaded device. A click, and I could send two inches of razor steel into your spinal column."

"That kill him straightaway?" asked Gus.

"Possibly. More likely, it would leave him paralyzed."

"So he wouldn't feel nothin'? No pain?"

"Why, Gus, old chap, am I detecting another possible experiment in the making?"

"Listen to me—" Travis said.

The cane pressed harder. "Apologies, constable, but I rather think not. Rest assured, if you shout, or attempt any . . . how do they phrase it? sudden moves? yes, I believe so . . . any sudden moves, and you'll be as good as dead from the collarbones down."

"So," said Gus, hunkering to study Travis with an intrigued look, "seems to me, like, if'n you tended the initial wound, a fella could live a fair long time."

"Oh, years, with proper care and adequately supplied fluids and nutrients," Bertrand said.

"Seems also to me a fella might not want to live like that."

"Wouldn't be much he could do about it, now, would there?"

"Stop eatin' and drinkin', I suppose."

"If his nurses allowed it. Or, if they took pity on him, and helped him along."

"You're insane, the both of you," Travis rasped.

"Oh, quite," Bertrand said. "Part of our charm."

"We all of us are," added Gus, "to some degree or t'other. Me and Bertrand here, we're not full-on maniacs like the Redwolf boys . . . we don't go around drownin' babies to watch 'em bubble, the way Tubber does . . . and, as for Horsecock . . . "

Bertrand tutted. "Please, Gus, the less said about him the better. There are Nasty Bastards, and then there are . . . *nasty* bastards."

Something wrong in his town, he'd thought? Trouble, he'd thought?

He'd had no damn idea!

The Nasty Bastards? *Here?* In Silver River?

An Injun raid would have been better! War-cries and scalpings and houses burnt to the ground were *nothing* compared to what he'd heard tell of the Nasty Bastards doing!

"Anyhow," Gus went on, "you, lawman, and these'uns, should count yourselves some lucky it was us you run into. You get a chance to do somethin' *meaningful* with your deaths. Advancin' the cause of science."

"If you're going to kill us, just get it over with!" He saw Nan's shock, but Nan didn't know, didn't understand. A quick end was the best they could hope for now.

"Hardly scientific," Bertrand said. "There's such knowledge to be gained. The tenacity of life truly is quite fascinating. We've conducted extensive research, compiling our results. I daresay there'll be a scholarly treatise in it someday. For instance, Sheriff, in your career, you must have observed or participated in executions. Hangings, let's say."

"Not enough," Travis growled, still hoping to provoke. "Got a couple more yet to see to."

Gus chortled. "The balls on him, how do you like that? Pinned down and helpless, tough-talking us."

"One does have to admire the rugged American frontier spirit."

"Lemme ask you, though, lawman . . . " Gus hunkered closer. "Little nowhere town like this, you the sort ended up here a disconsolate loser sunk in a whiskey bottle 'cause no other place would take you? Or the sort who used to be hot shit but got sick of the killin' and thought it'd be easy to settle somewheres quiet and see out the rest of your days with your feet up?"

"Gus, if I may interrupt? I'd not yet finished my

line of inquiry."

"Why, by all means, your lordship, and pardon the fuck out of me." Gus stood, tucking Travis' gun through the back of his belt. He bowed with a ridiculously fussy grandiosity. "Do carry on, pip pip, cheerio."

"Upon further consideration," Bertrand said, "let us abandon both lines of inquiry as irrelevant and proceed to our main purpose."

"You—" Travis began.

"Enough. Did I not say?" His words were followed by a sharp *click.*

And said sharp *click* followed by an equally sharp, equally brief flash of pain . . . followed by an utter numbness, a deadness of the flesh so complete it was as if his body had ceased to exist.

Panic spurred him, panic with no-damn-where to go and no-damn-good to do. Couldn't feel his arms, his legs, anything but the vaguest sensation of a rapid, padded thudding he suddenly knew to be his own heart, pumping frantically in the core of his chest. Doing its job, pulsing blood through his veins, for all the help it was.

"Aw, shit, Bertrand," Gus said. "What'd you do that for already?"

Couldn't feel, couldn't move, any part of him below the collarbones. Just as Bertrand had predicted. His lungs also somehow kept to their business, drawing and blowing dry gasps of air. A harsh whisper was all that escaped his lips.

"He'd've given us difficulties. And we do already have our two subjects for comparison. Help me heft him onto the table, there's a chap."

Travis barely comprehended as they lifted him. All

he could move was his head, side-to-side or up and down in jerky twitches . . . his eyes, flicking frantic . . . his jaw, his mouth working, throat straining for those harsh whispers—

"Bastards . . . paralyzed . . . " If he could raise his voice, raise the roof, raise the alarm! Something! Anything! Anything other than be unceremoniously heaved deadweight up from the floor and plopped onto a third table like a side of beef onto the butcher's block . . .

"I'll be damned," Gus remarked.

"Quite likely we all will, if our dear friend Josephiah has aught to opine on the matter."

"I don't mean Unholy Joe and us all bein' hellbound fer Satan. I mean, that nifty jabber of yourn really did fuck this here lawman up, din't it? He cain't feel a thing!" A grimy finger with a ragged nail poked Travis in the face. Best he could, he flinched away from it. "Felt that, though, din't'cha?"

"Fuck . . . you . . . "

They positioned him similar to how they had Nan and Charley, though in his case there was no need for strapping him down. His head lolled heavy, hanging over the table's edge, the simple effort to hold it level too much for him. From this skewed sideways vantage, he saw the room all catty-corner, saw Nan's tears and Charley's childlike terror as they kept on their futile squirming.

"Excellent," Bertrand said. Stepping back, he surveyed the scene, then consulted his pocketwatch. "Still with plenty of time. Shall we be to it?"

"Only if'n you promise to spare me the history lesson. Big ol' axes, swords for the queens, jumped-up Frenchie drop-blades . . . "

"Guillotines—"

"What-the-fuck-ever. Point is, we get the heads off. Sooner the better, one chop is best. No hackin' away or sawin'; takes too long."

Bertrand sniffed. "Fine, we'll dispense with the executioner's lore. If you're ready?"

They couldn't be doing this, this couldn't be happening! A bad dream, was all! He'd eaten something to disagree with him and it gave him the nightmares. Any moment, Travis knew, he'd wake up again. Only, for real this time, his earlier waking just a trick of his sleeping mind.

He'd wake up cold-sweats but safe, alone in his own bed, in his familiar room above the sheriff's office, and this would melt away like morning frost under a rising sun.

Any moment! Any moment, now!

He'd wake up, able to feel his body again, able to move his limbs. He wouldn't be lying here side-of-dead-beef as this dapper-suited bastard sat down primly at one of the smaller tables, pocketwatch in his left and pen in his right, the pen's nib poised over a ledger turned to a fresh page. He wouldn't be watching the other bastard selecting a cleaver, making a few experimental swipes with it, and turning to Nan and Charley.

"Which you think first?" Gus asked. "The woman or the ree-tard?"

"Either or," Bertrand said, pen scritching notes. "I suppose it'd be rude to keep the lady waiting."

"You . . . goddamn . . . " groaned Travis.

"Hold y'self steady," Gus told Nan as she squirmed

in the straps. "Wouldn't want to make a messy job of it."

Her bulging, pleading eyes met Travis'. Gus spat in his palms, rubbed them, and hoisted the largest cleaver from the Cookpot's kitchen. Its honed edge shone bright. So very, very bright. Vivid. Too vivid for dream-detail.

"One clean chop—" began Bertrand.

"I know, I fuckin' know, used to do this on chickens all the damn time."

"Nan!" Travis wheezed.

Whoosh and *chunk-thunk*, down the blade came. Crunching through neck-bone, shearing through flesh, burying itself in the tabletop with a decisive wood-splitting whack. Nan's head, hair pinned up in coiled bedtime-braids, fell right off the suddenly-red-and-gouting stump of her neck. Her body bucked once, a mighty heave so as to jolt the table. Her head dropped neat-as-you-please into the dish basin placed below.

Gus bent and sank his fingers into the mass of braids and coils, lifting her head like some fella from one of those crazy old Greek-style stories. Her eyes were still bulging, still pleading, still horribly *alive*, darting this way and that in desperate urgency. Her mouth gaped in a terrible, grimacing, silent scream.

Even had he been able to move just then, Travis wouldn't have been able to move. Wouldn't have been able to speak, or do anything but stare in absolute shock. Blood drizzled from Nan's severed head. Blood poured from her limp body in gushing and then slowing gurgles, like wine from an uncorked and tipped-over bottle.

Her eyes darted and pleaded. Seeing. Knowing.

Conscious. Alive.

Gus waved his other hand in front of them. "Ma'am? Can you hear me, ma'am? Blink twice if'n you can hear and understand me."

She glared at him with a hot-burning intensity.

"Not a blink," Bertrand observed, making notes, "but I do daresay she heard and understood you."

"Still there? Still with us? C'mon, give us a blink, a wink?" Gus shook Nan's head a little, grinning a jackal's encouraging grin. "Somethin'?"

Useless attempts at profanity were the best Travis could manage to sputter. Neither man paid him any mind, their attention fixed on Nan. When, at last, her face slackened and her eyes rolled glassy-blank, when her jaw sagged loose with tongue partway protruding, Bertrand pressed the button at the top of his pocketwatch.

"Six seconds," he announced, *scritchy-scratch* with the pen.

Gus looked from head to body. "And did you see how she thrashed there right at the start? If we hadn't strapped her down, she might well've gone strutting and flapping around like a chicken."

"You . . . woman-killers . . . " Travis said. "Cowards."

"Ain't that cute? Mister lawman trying to insult us." Gus dandled Nan's head in front of Travis. "Wouldn't you rather say a nice goodbye? Maybe give her a kiss?"

"Gus, please," Bertrand said. "Moving on."

"Fine, moving on." He tossed the head idly into the basin with no more care than he might've shown a cabbage. "Me, my money's on the ree-tard. He'll beat six seconds, easy."

"What makes you so sure?" asked Bertrand. "Women have often been known to demonstrate incredible tenacity and endurance under *extremis*. Witness childbirth, for example."

"Hell, no." Gus shuddered. "Walked in on that once, weren't nothin' normal nor natural about it. Miracle of life, my ass. No, me, I 'spect the ree-tard will be too plain dumb stupid to realize he's dead. Ten seconds, maybe twelve, I say."

"Rubbish. Seven at the very most."

"Yeah? Put a hundred on it?"

"Very well. A hundred it is."

"Now we're goddamn talkin'!"

All this while, poor halfwitted Charley had shivered on the table, face tucked under and eyes shut, as if he could make them not see him by account of him not seeing them. He jerked in the straps when Gus clapped him on the shoulder.

"All right, boy, I got good money on you, so don't you let me down. Can you talk? Answer me if'n you can talk."

"I wanna go bed," Charley mumbled.

"Be all done with real soon now. Here we go."

"Same chopper," suggested Bertrand. "Consistency, so as not to muddle the results."

"Naw, I thought I'd have his head off with a butterknife for some variety," Gus said. "Of course same damn chopper. You just mind your pocketwatch."

"Tick-tock. Jolly good."

Another *whoosh*, another *chunk-thunk*, another crunching through bone and shearing of flesh, and it was poor Charley's head plunking into the other dish-bin. Poor Charley's head being pulled up by the hair, held in mid-air before Gus's expectant gaze. Charley's confused eyes blinking, his mouth downturned and sorrowful.

"You hear me, boy? Say somethin', if'n you can hear me. What was it you wanted? To go to bed?"

"Buh . . . " A spitbubble swelled and burst on his lips.

"Hot damn, Bertrand, you see that? He talked!" Gus patted Charley's cheek. "That a boy! Hot damn!"

The corners of Charley's mouth twitched ever so slightly, as if even this absurd praise in this monstrous moment was worth a grateful smile. Then all signs of life and light and intelligence, murky though they were, drained from him along with the dregs of blood seeping thick from his neck.

"Eleven! Eleven at least; I counted!" crowed Gus.

"Eight seconds, by my watch."

"Eight, bullshit!"

They fell to dispute, bickering. Travis reckoned it was too much to hope that they'd come to blows. Just as it was too much to hope for reprieve or rescue.

Hell, but why would he *want* reprieve or rescue? Live out the rest of his life like *this*? Helpless and paralyzed? Needing constant nursing? Unable to feed himself, wipe himself?

No, the best he might have left to hope for was revenge, and even that hope seemed slim. *He* was the damn sheriff! For all he knew, the rest of Silver River could already be dead.

"Fine" said Gus; Travis had evidently missed part of their exchange. "Split the difference, call it fifty. My ree-tard did last the longer."

"Fine. Fifty it is, but I'll thank you to not further impugn the punctuality of my timepiece."

"Fine."

Fifty dollars went handed over from Bertrand to Gus. Then, after an indifferent wipe of the cleaver's bloodied blade, Gus strode up to the third table. He slanted a wicked grin Bertrand's way.

"Double-or-nothin'?"

"Ha, I say, ha."

"You'll swing for this," Travis whispered as best he was able.

"Like we ain't heard that before. Now, let me just shift your head over this-a-ways a tad . . . wouldn't want you to miss and go bouncing across't the floorboards."

"Unless we set up a ninepins," Bertrand said.

Gus laughed. "Maybe next time. Always got to find new ways t'keep it interestin'!"

He tried to shut them out, tried to ignore them. Tried to ignore the sensation of grimy-greasy blood-tacky fingers as Gus brushed aside his hair to expose the back of his neck . . . would've rather had worms and roaches crawling on his skin than that loathsome touch. Somehow, worst of all, was when the fingers passed below where Bertrand's cane-blade had skewered him . . . he knew they were there, but felt only numbness and a vague pressure.

"Any last words, constable?" Bertrand inquired politely. "Or might you favor us with a more detailed account of your experience, some few seconds from now? Being of sterner constitution and intellect than these others, as it were, I'd think you could elucidate with greater enlightenment."

"Fuck's sake, Bert, if'n you'd rather *talk* him to death, just say so."

Travis shut his eyes and composed his features as stoic as he was able, not wanting to give them the slightest satisfaction. He couldn't, however, shut his ears, or close off his remaining senses. He heard Gus raise the cleaver. The table's edge scraped the undershelf of his chin. His nose was beset by the stench of blood and loosed bowels.

His own loosed bowels?

He heard the *whoosh* of sharpened steel sweeping fast through the air. Heard a crunch, felt a jolt, and was abruptly *falling*.

The world flipped. He sucked in a breath, or tried to. His eyes popped back open, showing him a revolving blur from an insane perspective. A hard surface struck the top of his head. Everything rocked and wobbled.

Was it raining? A warm rain, wet and . . . red.

He came to rest on his right ear, but before he could clear his mind, the grimy fingers were upon him again.

Sinking into his hair, gripping a fistful, lifting his head . . . turning it . . . turning it so he was face to face with Gus. Up close and personal. Too close. Too personal.

"Well, mister lawman?"

Travis blinked. He saw Bertrand, observing intently, pocketwatch in one hand, poised pen in the other. He saw the three tables, the three headless bodies, the blood.

One of the bodies looked all too familiar, though

he'd never seen it—or expected, or wanted to—from this angle before.

"Well?" Gus repeated. "Any enlightenments or eee-lucidations for us?"

Travis spit square in his eye.

Then he was falling again, tumbling, as Gus dropped him.

The last thing he heard before impact and blackness was Bertrand saying, "My, my . . . Gus, old chap, I believe we have a new record."

4

SCENES FROM A MASSACRE

THE FUNNIEST THING about drownin' babies, in Tubber's view, was how dang plumb *bewildered* they got.

Especially when he un-dunked 'em a few times in the process. Hold 'em under, pull 'em up, watch 'em flail and sputter. All indignant, with the not-knowin' what the blue heck was going on.

Olden folks, too, if'n they were senile enough. But babies, babies always gave him such a chuckle!

Some easier to handle, too, babies were. Olden folk could be scrappy in a pinch. Even so confused by the dementia to forget their own names or so pained by the arthritis or other ailments you'd think they'd be glad to go, when push came right down to shove, they'd sometimes fight like the feisty dickens.

The babies never did. Didn't yet have the notions of self-defense, self-preservation. Didn't so much as occur to them. They plain couldn't understand, and it sure struck him funny. Every time.

This one, he'd scooped from its cradle while Shilo

and Jessie took care of the rest of the bakery family. Roly-poly little cherub, it was, chubby and pink, with a sweet dumpling face. Smelled like a fresh buttermilk biscuit. Slept like an angel, too, blissful and blameless, dreaming its baby dreams of milky tits and lullabies. Slept, even as he gathered it, swaddlin' blankets and all, into his arms.

Fussed a bit, no more than that. Scrunched its rosebud mouth in a moment's disturbance, blatted a faint complaint. Then, thumb found mouth, and back to baby dreamland it had gone.

Admittedly, he knew, taking it from the home was a risk. Toting it through town, more of a one. Better to have done the deed then and there. Had been a washtub in the kitchen perfect adequate to serve.

A bathhouse, though? A good and proper bathhouse? Where he could get a real immersion going?

How was a man to resist?

"That brat starts in crying, I'll wring its fat neck," Shilo had warned. "Nate wants us t' keep the noise down."

"I know, I know," Tubber had replied, rocking his warm cuddly armful. "But we're headed there next anyway, ain't we? Shame to waste a golden opportunity."

"Why you gotta do stuff like this?" asked Jessie. "Poor babe. Cutie, too."

"Cutie, nothin'," Shilo said. "Looks like a ham. And don't you go getting any ideas, woman. Last you need is a baby."

"Did I say as I wanted a baby? I did not. Only said how this one is a cutie. That wee nub of a nose—"

"Shit. This is how it starts. This is how it always

starts. What next, you'll be wanting to get hitched?"

"If ever I did, it wouldn't be to you! Ugly fuck."

"Sassmouth cow."

He grabbed his crotch at her, and she slapped her ass at him, and Tubber just rolled his eyes. "I'll keep the kid quiet," he'd said.

Which, for the most part, he had, except when he set it down so's he could fill the tub. Unlikely, though, the sound carried far. Hadn't lasted long, neither. Not once Tubber returned his attention to the baby.

Unwrapping it from its swaddlin', he cooed and made funny faces and did the sing-song nonsense. Soon, he had it smiling. Grabbing at his fingers. Trying to suckle on his pinkie the way it had its own thumb.

Sweetie cherub dumpling, really was. Cute as could be.

The cold water must've come as a shock. Made Tubber himself gasp, submerged as he was to the elbows. Being plunged full right into it with a hearty splash, plunged right in and held right down . . . oh, yes, must've been a shocker indeed!

Oh, but look at it go, just wavin' its little arms, pedalin' its pudgy legs! Trying to swim, going nowhere fast.

Tubber laughed. "Slippery, squirmy cuss, ain't ya?"

He brought it up, let it flail and sputter, dunked it again. Bubbles streamed from both ends. Dunk and splash, lift and thrash, cold water droplets flying every whichway, the tub's surface roiling with ripples.

And there it was, *there*, the bewildered look! Utter incomprehension. What was happening? What . . .

how . . . why?

Dunk and hold.

Hold. Hold, as the squirming first intensified to fever-pitch, then stilled. Hold, as the small plump body went rigid in his hands. As the bubbles trailed off. As the rigid body relaxed again. As the surface grew smooth, and fine wisps of hair floated a halo around the cherub's sweet little head.

Its agog eyes sought some understanding forever beyond their reach.

Not angry, not afraid, the way the olden folks sometimes were.

Just so very bewildered.

One final bubble arose, the tiniest silvery wavering *plip*.

He never got tired of it. Funniest darn thing he ever did see.

Welp, that was it . . . Death done come to Silver River. All this time folk's'd been sayin' the town was on its last legs, dyin' and such, but Milo Dunnings never did think it would happen like this. No, sirree. He sure never did.

Death come in the night. Like a plague, but not the smallpox or cholera kind. More the kind like what the preacher talked about, like in Egypt, dark angels moving door to door in silent slaughter.

Hadn't he seen it with his very own eyes?

Peculiar, though, how Death's dark angels resembled regular men. Or maybe they as chose it that way on purpose. Wouldn't do, going forth fierce and fearsome, crowned in thorns of fire.

Or sommat-the-sort. He couldn't quite remember. Furthermore, he was drunk. Drunk even by his own ain't-had-but-a-few standards. Too drunk t' go home. Ashamed t' go home, that hangdog-drunk where he couldn't bear the prospect of reeling on in, puke-sick and stinking, a right disgraceful mess. Upsetting his wife. Frightening the lil'uns. Making his Daisy-girl give him that *look* what she gave.

Lord, no, he could not bear that *look*.

Not tonight. Not ever again, please and praise God.

Let this here be it. Let it be over. Death done come to Silver River, Death with dark angels. Reaper-scythes in the shape of knives, ending lives.

That were some poetic, and he wished he could write it down. He'd forget by morning. Only, there wouldn't be no more mornings for him, or for anyone else in this town. When the sun rose, it'd rise to slit throats and stabbed hearts, to necks snapped and strangled, to lopped-off heads. To blood. So much blood.

He did know. He had seen it. Stumbling around, peering bleary through windows. Folks dead in their beds and him down to the dregs of a bottle. Be his turn soon enough. A dark angel would find him and put a sharp end to the wretchedness he'd become.

Should he maybe go on home after all? Be with his wife and lil'uns? Let Death take the lot of them together, as a family?

Should he, as a final effort to do right by them, spare them the waiting? Spare them the fear? Put an end to their poverty and misery, which he had caused? Didn't he owe them that much, at least?

It'd be easy enough, for the most part. His wife bein' so poorly, so weak. And the lil'uns . . . they'd be sound asleep . . . even a drunken waste like him could hardly make a botch of that.

Only his Daisy-girl, he reckoned, might pose him a problem. He'd just have to do for her first.

Resolved, but with tears prickling the corners of his eyes, Milo Dunnings headed for home.

Nate Bast, the original Nasty Bastard himself, hummed softly as he emerged from the mayor's house, wiping his bloodied hands on a rag.

The actual looting and mop-up work, he could leave to his underlings. Rank had its privileges and all.

He refreshed with a swig from his hip-flask, rocking back and forth on his bootheels as he surveyed, with some satisfaction, the surrounding town.

Kind of nice, doing it this way. On the quiet. An interesting change of pace from riding in hootin'-and-hollerin' hellbent for leather with guns a'blazin.

Though, of course, that approach *did* also have its merits. Quick, crazy, like an Indian raid, smash and grab and shoot and burn, and be long gone before anybody might muster up resistance or pursuit.

This more subtle way, it took longer, and it required more planning and discipline—the latter being a characteristic some of his gang rather tended to lack—but it also meant a more thorough acquisition of rewards.

And, hey, if it gave his more . . . eccentric . . . followers an opportunity to indulge their . . . whims . . . well, so much the better. Helped to keep them happy. Wouldn't do to let them get too disgruntled.

Speaking of disgruntled, however, he supposed he could expect no small amount of complaining later. Silver River was hardly overflowing with wealth. Still, they'd turn a decent sum when all was said and done.

Particularly with the twin girlies, the mayor's daughters or nieces. If not the prettiest, they were at least a matched set. That had to fetch a little something extra. It'd be a hassle to transport them, always was, but worth the effort. The two were currently trussed up like turkeys, barefoot and bare-headed in their night-dresses, too shock-struck to cry but gagged just in case.

Rest of the household, mayor included? Dead as the proverbial door-nails, without putting up much of a fight. The hired man might've made a difference, had he not been so stone drunk he'd never even stirred.

True to form, the mayor hadn't wanted to give up the combination to his safe, so a touch of persuasion had been necessary. Only a touch, though. Amazing how cooperative a fella could become after a few little cuts. You'd think he'd lost a limb, the way he carried on.

Too bad the safe had then proved something of a disappointment. More debt-papers than dollars. Seemed Mr. Mayor—as was typical of the political-type breed—had been involved in some shady land dealings. Even trying to bribe the railroad folks into reconsidering their plans. Who knew? Few years hence, maybe he'd've put Silver River back on the map.

Well, no chance of it now. Gone a right gusher, he had. Same for his dull-eyed sister and weasel-faced brother-in-law. Small wonder the girlies were shock-struck.

Nate took another swig, grinning. Town was as good as theirs. With still no shots fired, no screams screamed. Very little in the way of noise or disturbance, all considered. Unholy Joe hadn't even set fire to the church, yet.

He wondered how Dex and the Redwolf boys were getting on, over to the east end of the valley. And ol' Horsecock, who'd gone alone to a homestead up by the hills; he always did take his sweet time, perverted deviant that he was.

To think, Nate's own sister had gone and *thanked* him, after . . .

As if mental mention of the man's name had summoned the man himself, there he was, riding into view down the moonlit street. At a leisurely canter, he came over to Nate, dipping his head in a nod and touching his hatbrim.

"Finished early, did you?" Nate asked, then rather wished he hadn't for fear Horsecock would feel obliged to share the details.

Instead, he just shrugged. "Seems they weren't much my sort. 'Sides, found something might ought interest you."

"Oh, yeah?" He eyed the loot-sack slung from

Horsecock's saddle. "Good haul?"

"Huh? Nah, some cash, some silver, nice pewter picture-frame, such and like. But, here. Take you a gander at this."

What he proffered was hardly a thick wad of money or fist-sized nugget of gold. Was just a piece of paper, a handbill such as would be posted in a shopkeep's window. Which, it occurred to Nate, he'd seen a few of already but paid them no particular mind. Now, he did.

DOCTOR ODDICO'S CARNIVAL OF ODDITIES AND MUSEUM OF MARVELS! it proclaimed.

Nate read it, then shot Horsecock a wry eyebrow. "The hell you tellin' me? You want to go to the circus?"

"Naw."

"Run off and *join* the circus, then? Take up showin' your piece there for ten cents a look?"

Horsecock rolled his eyes. "Point is, see how it says Friday and Saturday? And this Lost Meadow can't be too far from here. Which means—"

"Which means," Nate said, catching the train, "these carnival folk are probably already there, getting set up."

"Right. Could cause us a complication."

"Orrr . . . could cover our tracks. We just make it look like they were the ones what did this, and we're well on our way with no one the wiser."

"Wasn't you planning to let them weird-god hill people take the blame? The, what'd'ya call 'em, Truthies?"

"Something like that, some freak cult or another, marry their own daughters or the like. But, Joe says they're too peaceable for an outright attack. Besides, he'd just as soon go after them next."

"Accourse he would," Horsecock said. "Man's right-up insane."

Nate thought *pot-and-kettle* at that, but weren't about to say so. He rolled various possibilities around in his head. "Now, these carnies, though, they might have a fair bit of coin. You know how they are, that sort. Cheats and thieves to a one. Telling fortunes, selling snake-oil, running rigged games of chance."

"Could also be ready for trouble, them, though," Horsecock said. "Moreso than an unsuspecting townful of reg'lar people or peaceable culties."

"Well, we'll finish up here and then decide." Nate swept the town another surveying glance. "You want the schoolhouse next?"

"Some old-maid schoolmarm? Nah. What else?"

"Post office, or, I'm heading over to the lawyer's place. Mister Mayor let blab a few secrets while I was cutting on him, and it seems the lawyer's missus come into a tidy little inheritance recently."

"Lawyer's got a missus, huh?"

"Hell." Nate sighed. "Fine, you go on ahead. Just make sure you get the damn money, willya?"

Still half-asleep, Lacy shifted onto her side and reached out . . . but found the other side of the bed empty.

Again?

He'd promised to stay. Promised this time he

would. That they'd snuggle together all night, like spoons in a drawer. His back against her bosom, or her bottom against his loins . . . arms draped over each other . . . legs interlaced . . . skin-to-skin naked . . . slow-breathing the mingled scents of their sex.

All night, he'd assured her, murmuring into her hair, kissing her ear, holding her close. All night, and then they'd rise and dress and go downstairs together. Give her boss the news first.

Would hardly be a surprise; Sam Harlowe himself had been the one to tell Lacy he knew her days of whoring would soon be numbered. Not so much call for it in Silver River these days. She poured drinks at the Bell more often than she turned tricks anymore. Not due to any deterioration in her appearance, that was for sure; she hadn't gone fat or got scarred up or fallen to haggard habits the way some girls did.

It was just, Sam had observed, with his avuncular kindness, that her heart didn't seem to be in it as much. Business had tapered as fewer and fewer travelers passed through town. And her regular local customers had begun gradually withdrawing their custom once it was noticed . . . her and J.B.

"It's our very own love story," Canna McCall liked to say. Lordy, but the would-be newswoman had a flair for the dramatic. "The strapping young deputy, the soiled dove, against all odds and obstacles . . ."

Lacy didn't know for all that, star-crossed lovers and whatnot. Maybe some feared J.B. would prove the possessive, jealous type. Fly into a rage if he saw her so much as talking to another man.

Or, more likely, they'd just thought—like Sam did, and Canna—she and J.B. really did make a good match. Felt they belonged together. Wished them well. A happily-ever-after in the waiting.

She herself sure wouldn't object. True, she'd had her qualms at first, about getting involved beyond her usual. But J.B. was different. J.B. was special. He didn't care about her past, or what Preacher Gaines had to say about harlots and fallen women, or what his kinfolk might think, or what consorting with a whore might do to his career aspirations.

He loved her.

Said he did, at least. And gave her cause to believe him . . . most of the time.

Then there were nights like this. When, despite his talk and his promises, she'd wake to find him gone. Overrun by guilt, or duty, or righteousness, or doubt.

Lacy sighed and buried her face in his pillow. He couldn't have been gone long; his warmth lingered. Had she been roused by the click of the door as he closed it behind him? Or the tread of his boots descending the stairs?

A thump from elsewhere in the building gave her pause to reconsider. Maybe he'd only gone for a piss, or something to drink.

Hiking herself up on an elbow, she looked around the room. On a chair, in a patch of moonlight, hung his gunbelt. Right where he'd hung it when they went to bed. His hat was there, too. And his vest, with its tin deputy star.

So, he hadn't left her again, hadn't done the shameful slink back to the sheriff's office. He'd never have left his hat, badge, and gun.

Relief washed through her. A piss or a drink, or some other errand, was all. He'd return soon enough.

Return, to find his lovely Lacy waiting.

To that end, she adjusted her pose on the bed to her best comely advantage. Twining the sheet around herself to expose a smooth length of thigh, she tousled her hair so it spilled in fetching tumbles over her breasts.

Minutes went by, with still no J.B. She heard the familiar creaks and groans of settling wood; the Silver Bell was well-constructed, but every building had its telltales when someone was up and about.

Were those voices? A hushed conversation? Sam suffered sometimes from insomnia, occasionally sitting up half-'til-dawn playing solitaire. She craned an ear. Was he down there chatting with J.B.?

She slid from the bed and into a robe, then padded barefoot to her door for a closer listen. As soon as she did, the voices ceased, and she had the strangest sensation of someone listening as intently for her as she was for them. As if whoever was below had heard her gentle footfalls, and gone silent in fear of discovery.

Imagination running away with her? At this rate, she'd rival Mrs. McCall for dramatic flairs.

Chiding herself, she ventured out into the hall. A lone lamp burned at the top of the stairs, doing more to spread shadows than really cast light. But Lacy, having worked at the Silver Bell since she was sixteen, would've known her way blindfold.

At the railing, she paused to peer over. The saloon floor was a pool of darkness, offering only mere suggestions of the long bar with its shelves of bottles, the gaming tables, and the piano corner.

From this angle, she couldn't see to the back,

where Sam's rooms were. She moved to the head of the stairs. Immediately, the lamplight behind her threw her own shadow looming large.

"Sam?" she said softly, taking a downward step.

The intently-listening silence was the only answer.

"Sam?"

Another step, and more silence.

"Mr. Harlowe? Are you awake?"

Hand grazing the banister, robe's hem swishing at her ankles.

"J.B.?"

As she neared the bottom few steps, her foot encountered something not made of staircase. Something warmer and more yielding than wood.

Lacy held absolutely still. Part of her wanted to turn and race up the stairs, to her room, where she'd slam the door lock it hide under her bed. Part of her wanted to crouch and explore by touch what she could of the huddled shape on the steps, confirming or refuting a dreadful suspicion. Part of her wanted to leap over it and run for the exit, screaming her head off as she burst through the bell-shaped batwing doors.

"J.B.?" she whispered.

Ever so slowly, so terribly slowly, she crouched. Her fingertips met flesh. Warm, but inert. Flesh, and skin. Skin that, she feared, had most recently been pressed naked against her own.

"Oh, J.B., oh no—"

Rough hands shot unseen from the dark and seized her. Even as her mouth opened to scream, an icy line sliced across her neck. Sliced fast, and sliced deep. The iciness was replaced by a torrential wet heat coursing over her breasts.

She felt her knees buckle, felt herself begin to fall, but never felt the landing.

"Yea, though an apple may appear pristine but within harbor gruesome worms of decay, so too may the white walls of God's own house conceal the vilest rot and corruption."

The walls indeed were white, freshly whitewashed. The steeple rose tall. Panes of colored glass composed the arched windows. The steps were stone, the path to them of neatly-raked gravel.

"What sins dwell find here? What sins of the Seven? Is there undue Pride taken in this fineness of structure? Envy of churches in neighboring towns, for larger congregations or finer trappings?"

The tidiness of the building, well-kept and in good repair, suggested the absence of Sloth . . . but that might be the work of some hard-pressed hireling, back bent in daily toil for pittance wages, while God's special servant himself did precious little physical labor.

"Does Greed live within, the collection plate a hungry mouth to fatten the coffers rather than help the needy and poor? As for hungry mouths, what of Gluttony? In the larder, will humble fare be found, or rich feasting?"

Rare to meet a skinny priest, in Josephiah's experience. Rare, indeed. Well-fed, they were, and soft-handed. Living large, cush and comfortable, by the generosity of those hoping to bribe their way into forgiveness.

"For they speaketh much of Wrath to incite fire and hatred in the hearts of others, but taketh not up the sword themselves. In this, too, do they benefit unearned, set safe in peace and righteousness while blood is shed!"

How quick they were to claim the protection of their office! Let thieves be hanged, witches be burned, let children die and innocents suffer . . . but, 'pon threat and pain of damnation, let no harm befall so much as a hair upon a preacher-man's anointed head!

"And Lust? Does Lust have a home within this hallowed house? Does the shepherd's eye rove with lasciviousness o'er his sheep, even as his lips decry adultery and fornication?"

Oh, probably, Josephiah knew. Whether acted on or not, the Serpent's whisper tickled many a pious ear. Often tantalizing not even just with normal lusts, but those most dark and twisted. Unnatural. Depraved.

To be fair, he had in his time run across a few who did practice as they preached, who were earnest in their faith. Most, though? Hypocrites. Hypocrites to the core. Not that it mattered much either way. He'd dispatch them all the same.

For so his Master wished it.

He let himself into the church by way of the front door. The handle did not sear his skin. He did not burst aflame when he crossed the threshold. Lightning did not strike him down as he made his way between the rows of pews.

There was no angelic outcry when he pissed upon the pulpit, or squatted to shit at the foot of the cross.

None when he took from his satchel a festering rat corpse and slapped it onto the open pages of the waiting Bible. None when he opened a jar of goat's blood and smeared the Devil's mark on every wall and window.

No divine intervention when he went into the attached parsonage at the church's rear, found the preacher sleeping the contented sleep of the smugly complacent—well-fed and soft-handed, as expected—and dragged him from his bed.

Hyacinth was close to foaling. Her first time, and she was skittish, which meant not much in the way of rest for Abram Scott that night.

He'd made himself a spot in the next stall over, reading by candlelight when not checking on and talking soothing to the young mare. Or, trying to; her nervousness had set his own nerves fair on edge as well. He kept jumping at shadows and twitching at sounds, until he felt more akin to someone standing watch at the graveyard than waiting midwife to a horse. Could hardly concentrate, must've re-read the same page six times over now without a sentence sinking in.

When he heard stealthy noises outside the stable, he almost dismissed it as nothing more than the wind, or someone passing by on a very late errand. Or one of his uncles, come to see how Hyacinth was doing. Or his little brother Albert, trying to sneak back in after his earlier clandestine sneaking-out.

But, his jumpy nerves insisted it was none of those

things. His jumpy nerves prompted him to blow out the candle with a puff of breath, and wait quiet in the hay-smelling dark.

Was it voices? The low mutter of voices in some sort of debate? Seemed like . . . had a *you-do-this-and-I'll-do-that* quality, not quite argument and not quite order.

Couldn't be horse-thieves, could it? Rustlers? In Silver River? Hardly seemed worth the effort, out-of-the-way as they were. Didn't have more than a dozen in town, all told, and half of those stabled out at Cottonwoods Ranch anyway.

Whatever it was, there went his nerves again, even further on edge.

Hyacinth's, too; she huffed and snorted, shifting her ungainly swollen bulk from hoof to hoof. A few of the others answered her with huffs and snorts and shifts of their own, impatient-like, as if telling her she was only having a foal, it was nothing to get her withers in a bunch over.

No, it *was* voices, Abram felt sure of it. Unfamiliar ones. None of his uncles or neighbors would come creeping around the livery at any rate, and it could hardly be Albert.

He keened his ears to listen past Hyacinth's fussing.

Yes, there they were. Voices, two or three of them. Men's voices.

Unfamiliar voices . . .

. . . and unfriendly.

Using *that* word.

Abram knew *that* word, all right. His momma didn't even let his grandpappy say it in the house, and the sole time Abram had said it himself within her earshot, she'd smacked him 'crost the face with a wet dishcloth.

But here were some strangers in the middle of the night, using it disparaging as they crept around the stable. Along with other words that often accompanied it, words such as 'dirty,' 'damn,' and 'uppity.'

Genuine fear piled onto his nerves then, fear for more than the possible loss of their livelihood. The war may have been over; some sentiments remained unchanged.

He groped for and found the handle of a pitchfork he'd left leaning after spreading fresh hay for Hyacinth's stall. Even as his hand closed around it, he knew how much trouble he'd end up in if he had to use it. All that "created equal" might look good on paper, but if the likes of him harmed a white man— even a horse-thieving outlaw of a white man—he'd be strung up just as quick.

The stable door groaned open a crack. Abram saw a lone silhouette in the moonlight, an indistinct man-shape.

"No lights," the man-shape said. "Eyes must've been playing tricks on you."

"Could've sworn I saw—" another man replied.

"I tell you, there's nothing. Come on. Let's deal with these darkies and find someone *worth* killing." The man moved away, leaving the door indifferently ajar.

Abram stood rigid for a terrible moment, the faces of his family flashing through his mind. He could hide, and survive. He could run, and seek help. He could—

He could dash from the stable, pitchfork held in both fists, as the strangers approached the house. They had knives. Long knives, glinting deadly and sharp.

Abram charged at them just the same. The one bringing up the rear paused, cocking his head as if hearing something.

"Hold up," he said, and turned. "Thought I—"

The pitchfork tines punched into his belly far easier than they'd ever punched into a bale of hay. Fleshier. Meatier. Gooshier, somehow. Abram felt a giving, gelatinous quiver run up the wooden handle and into his arms. He saw the man's eyes widen, saw the man's mouth drop open, heard his blurt of surprise.

They stared at each other, and it was hard to say which of them was the more shocked. The impaled man swung wildly with his knife, but the length of the pitchfork kept him at too great a distance to cut anything more than air.

"I told you," began the first man, glancing back, "there was noth—"

Letting go of the knife, the impaled man drew his pistol, and fired.

Once, when he'd been helping his uncles shoe a cantankerous horse, Abram had the bad luck to take a kick to the ribs. Broke two of them. A jagged end had scraped, nearly puncturing, his lung. He'd coughed up red for a week, been wrapped in birchbark and bandages most of the summer and still had a half-moon scar to remind him.

Worst pain he'd ever known in his life . . . until

now, as his collarbone shattered and his shoulder exploded and he fell down screaming in an eruption of blood.

PART THREE:

HIGH MOON AT MIDNIGHT

1

SHOTS AND SCREAMS

CANNA McCALL started awake to find her husband already upright in bed beside her, gun in hand.

"Was that—?" she began.

Another shot split the night with an unmistakable crack before Shane had to provide an answer.

"Check the kids," he said as he swung his bad leg out from under the covers. "And get my rifle. I'll grab the shotgun."

She didn't fuss or argue, just sprang up straight away and dashed for the stairs. Flying up them, feet barely seeming to touch each riser, she heard the awful screaming from the direction of the livery come to an abrupt, even-more-awful, end.

Trouble at the saloon? Drunk men plus gambling plus weapons? Robbery? Murder? Had the shots been fired by Sheriff Travis? Outlaws? Indians? A busy bee-hive of questions and speculations buzzed in her mind, but she pushed them aside for the utmost important priority.

"Cody? Mina?" she called, not loud but in a carrying quiet urgency.

Upstairs weren't but a few small rooms, despite the post office's grander false-front facade. Dark, too, only thin lines of moonlight beaming in through the hall-end window's shutter-slats. The doors were all shut, neither of the children having yet poked their heads out . . . they'd be more apt to poke their heads out their windows instead, both being burdened with her curiosity and Shane's gumption.

Dread clutched her heart at the thought of some whiskey-stupid ranch-hands shooting wild, sending bullets who-knew-where. By the sounds of a rising clamor outside, whatever was happening was bigger than some saloon brawl gone wrong. She heard rough voices, vehement cussing, horrified cries.

The first shut door she reached was Cody's, and she flung it open to reveal . . . *what in the world?* A tousle-haired lump tucked snug and peaceful under the quilt? No *way* he'd sleep through—

"Cody?"

It took less than a moment for her to realize the deception, and the rest of the moment for comprehension to set in. A dummy of rolled blankets and woolly mat in the bed, because Cody, their Cody, wasn't in it at all. His day's clothes were not in their usual untidy pile, his boots gone from their usual place.

She ran to Mina's room next, mouth dry, pulse hammering. No deception awaited . . . but no Mina, either. The girl's bedclothes were rumpled, as if hastily thrown back into place after the girl herself vacated. Her night-dress hung draped on the back of a chair.

Down again Canna went, still flying, feet still not seeming to touch the stair risers. Passing through the sitting room, she paused only long enough to snatch the rifle from above the mantle. She found Shane in the vestibule dividing their living quarters from the post office—built large in the optimism of someday housing a telegraph apparatus and her newspaper printing press, though thus far used mainly for storage.

"Men in the street," he said. "Outlaw gang is my guess. Attacking the town—"

"The kids're gone!"

"What?" He whipped around to look at her sharply. "Gone?"

"Gone from their beds, the both of them. Cody left a dummy—"

"Hell-*fire* and damnation! Snuck out?"

"To Lost Meadow, I expect."

"That boy. That girl." Shane exhaled, taking the rifle, cracking it to check the load. "All right. Nothing we can do about it now."

"Maybe it's a good thing? Maybe they're safe out of town?"

"Maybe," he said, grim-like.

"You don't think *that's* them, do you? The carnival folk? Attacking?"

"Don't know. Here." He passed her shotgun, too. "Sure you can handle it?"

She nodded, because no other response would do. Familiar with its use, yes. Fired it into the air to scare off a brown bear once, yes. Pointed it at another person? She'd hoped that day would never come. Although worry for the children beat in her as fast as her pulse, a worry close to panic, she forced herself calm. If that day had come, she wasn't about to let her husband down.

"Go on and cut loose, boys!" a man shouted, outside in the street. "Announced our presence now, haven't we? Playtime's over; no more point being shy!"

A chorus of whoops, yee-haws, rebel yells and cheers greeted this proclamation. Mixed in with it were screams—terror, pain, anguish, rage. Among those were voices Canna recognized, including Hazel Scott from the livery wailing her boy Abram's name. Neighbors yelled for help, for the doctor, for the sheriff. Yelled that the church was on fire, that Mayor Fritt done been killed, that there'd been slaughters at the Silver Bell and the mercantile and at Nan's!

Torches flared. Shadows cavorted. Someone bashed open the post office's door, hollering, "Special delivery!" and three men crowded in, jeering and waving pistols, like they anticipated meeting no resistance.

Well, surprise on them, wasn't it?

Shane shot the first one between the eyes and blew a fair brain- and blood-laden portion of the back of his skull all over the faces of his comrades. Before they even knew what had happened, Canna pulled the trigger. The shotgun's roar blasted their legs out from under them. They went down in a tangled pile, one dead and two howling.

"Stay put!" Shane rushed forward. Bad leg or no, stiff-gaited hobble or no, he rushed forward to finish off the two wounded men.

"Love you too and hell I will!" Canna followed, racking the shotgun and chambering another round.

The man who'd shouted earlier shouted again. "The fuck's this? On your toes, boys; we got some live ones here!"

"We got some dead ones here!" Shane shouted back. "Step on up and we'll add to the pile!"

A fourth man—bold, foolish, or just plain with bad timing—appeared in the doorway right then.

"Down!" Canna said.

Shane dropped low. She aimed high. The shotgun roared again and obliterated the intruder from the collarbones up. Having never killed a man before, she supposed she ought to have been aghast, but as chunky red debris pattered wetly on the porch and his body collapsed like an unmoored scarecrow, all she felt was a vicious satisfaction.

More shouts and cussing came from outside. It seemed they were holding off, sizing up, taking it more strategic. Or . . .

"'Round back," Shane said. "Kitchen door. Mind the windows."

Canna went, and a part of her was indeed strangely glad that the children were gone. Wherever they *were*, she didn't know, and was heartsick with worry, but at least they weren't *here*. There'd have been no way on earth to keep them from trying to join in the fray, Cody with that slingshot of his, Mina apt to kick even a grown man three times her size. No, wherever they *were*, at least she could take some comfort in knowing they might be safe!

The kitchen door rattled even as she reached the

room. Locked, but the front latch hadn't held up and the back was no better. Canna crouched behind the table, took aim, and waited. She heard Shane's gun fire twice more—that was five, she'd kept count—and then a heavy bootheel thudded against wood and the kitchen door juddered open. Rather than leap aside for cover, two figures plunged through. She let the first one, a man, have it to the midsection. The blast damn near cut him in half, spreading his guts on the wall like strawberry jam.

The second, a woman, got off a shot of her own, but Canna's crouching saved her; the bullet passed above her, pinged off the stove and ricocheted into the ceiling. A second shot carved a splintery trench and buried itself in the thick slab tabletop.

Canna ducked even lower, under the table, peering through a forest of chair legs at the woman's grimy boots. Looked as if she'd tromped through a cow-barn on her way here, and Canna had the sudden mad urge to scold. *Wipe your feet, bitch; I don't even let my own children track that shit in my house!*

Instead, she again let the shotgun do the talking. Her ears rang so she barely heard the woman's agonized shriek as her right knee burst like a pine cone in the fireplace. The woman didn't fall, though; somehow she clung to the doorframe and stayed balanced on her left foot. But she'd lost hold of her revolver. It fell to the floor, and Canna—the shotgun now empty—went for it.

Scrabbling under the table on her hands and knees, shouldering chairs out of the way, she went for it.

Went for it, and got it. Got it, and used it. Firing

up at an angle, three times. Bang, bang, bang! Hitting the outlaw woman twice squarely—once in the stomach and once in the chest—and grazing her arm with the third as she wheeled, tottering, before losing her balance. She fell backward out the door.

Moving fast, burgeoning with a mad strength she'd never known herself capable of, Canna slammed the door and upended the table against it in a half-assed but sturdy kind of barricade. The man whose guts she'd blown out lay sprawled with the upper and lower portions of his body connected by maroon loops of gristle and a knobby twist of bone.

Again, all she felt was that vicious satisfaction. She grabbed his guns, too, scooped up the shotgun, and hurried to find Shane. He was still in the front business area of the post office, reloading, sheltered by the bulk of a desk. A respectable pile of bodies had built up in the open doorway. It didn't look like the bad guys were in a hurry to keep trying that approach, but neither did she think they were ready to give up. They'd be withdrawing to regroup, make a plan.

The firelight filtering in from the street had grown brighter, and not only from the torches. Something *was* burning, probably the church as had been said. Possibly other buildings as well . . . and, quite possibly, this building next.

She hunkered down beside Shane. Their eyes met in the hellish flickering gloom, gazes saying all as needed be said. He brushed the backs of his knuckles against her cheek. She turned her head to press into the touch. The ringing in her ears had begun to subside, letting other noises trickle in. Shouting. More gunfire. More screams. Shattering glass.

"They'll set fire the place," Shane said. "When they do, I'll cover your escape, but I'll need you to *run*."

"I can't leave you."

"You'll have to." He thumped a fist against his hip, where the old wound was, where shrapnel remained embedded deep in the bone. "We both know why."

"Shane—"

"Cody and Mina are out there somewhere. You run, you hide, and you find them. Don't fret over me." He caressed her cheek again, and she kissed his hand, blinking away her tears.

"Hey!" hailed the man who'd been shouting before. Must've been the one in charge, leader of the gang. "You at the post office, you still there?"

"Come on in and find out," Shane called.

"Look, now, I admit, you did cause me a problem. I wasn't countin' on losin' so many men. Even so, I got plenty more, and more on the way—" His voice fell briefly to a grumble, something *if-the-damn-maniacs-ever-fuckin'-get-here* something. "But you, you're 'bout out of allies and out of options. No need t' make this harder than it has to be. Your sheriff's dead—"

"Me an' Bert's got his head right here!" another man crowed. "Fifteen seconds, set us a record, he did!"

"—and so's his deputy. So's your mayor and your preacher and 'bout everyone else in this piss-pot excuse for a town. 'Cept for some of your coloreds, and a couple kids—"

"Kids!" Canna gasped, clutching at Shane's sleeve.

"Easy, now," he told her, though she felt his

muscles thrum with tension.

"—and maybe a few others we might've missed here and there. And you, mister. Who are you, anyways?"

"Just the postmaster."

"Beggin' your pardon, but I do kind of doubt that."

"Doubt all you like," Shane replied. After craning up quick for a glance, he leaned close to Canna and spoke low. "Be ready. They'll have the place surrounded. Out the side window, shoot anyone as gets in your way, and keep on going."

She drew a deep breath, holding the gutshot dead man's gun steady in both hands—it was full-loaded, she'd already checked—and nodded.

Shane raised his voice again. "Anyways, stranger, since you've held off to talk, what do you want?"

"Simple enough; to pack up our loot and be on our way, without you puttin' holes in any more of my gang. You agree to chuck out your guns and sit quiet, we won't have to have further bloodshed."

"Hmm. And, begging *your* pardon, but somehow *I* doubt *that*."

"Well, fair's fair, you c'n doubt all you like, too," the man said, chuckling. "I could give you my word, if'n it'd help."

"You could give me your name."

"Y'know, I could, but I've a feelin' it would only make you even less inclined to trust me."

"Yeah," Shane said. "Yeah, somehow I expect you're right."

"So, mister postmaster, what's it gonna be? We got us a deal? Or we got us an impasse?"

"Lemme think on it a minute!"

"Bertrand, you heard the man . . . mark us one minute, if you please."

"I did indeed," replied someone with a prissy British accent. "The clock is ticking."

To Canna, Shane whispered, "Spotted the bastard. He's by the schoolhouse. From the front window, I'll have a shot. Not the best, but a shot."

"Shane . . . "

"Be ready," he repeated. "I'll have their attention."

Giving her no further opportunity to object, he tucked the long rifle under his arm and rapid-crawled to the window, hauling his bad leg like a length of cordwood. At some point in the proceedings, two of the lower panes had been broken, shards twinkling on the floor, the edges of muslin half-curtains flapping.

Canna steeled herself and did her own crawl to the side window, the one that gave onto an alleyway between the post office and what had been a tobacconist/apothecary before the silver claims petered out and the owner decided he'd have better fortune in Winston City. The alleyway was weeds and dirt; she and Mina kept planning to put in a little garden, but neither of them had much patience for that sort of thing . . . and what was she doing, thinking about gardens right now? When she'd be lucky even to see her girl again?

"Thirty seconds," declared the British-accented Bertrand. "Tick-tock."

"You wouldn't be up to any mischief in there, would you, mister postmaster?" the leader called.

"I said I was thinking on it," Shane called back, bracing on his good knee and lifting the rifle into position. "What about the rest of the townsfolk? You gonna let them live, too?"

"Oh, we've had enough killing for one night, don't you agree?"

"Matter of fact, I don't."

If the shotgun had been a roar, the rifle was a whipcrack. As soon as she heard it, Canna heaved up the window, hiked her night-dress, and scrambled out. The scramble turned into a tumble, her fetching up flat on her back in the dirt.

"Ahhh, *fuck*!" the leader screamed, in considerable pain. "Fucker *shot* me!"

Then there was even more of a hell of a ruckus. Men swore and shouted. More gunfire barked and spat. Righting herself quick, Canna heard the rifle's whipcrack report again, amid the crash of breaking glass as someone hurled something—a torch? a brick?—through the post office front window.

Her heart seized, her husband's name at her lips. But she did what he'd wanted and took off at a run.

Shoot anyone that got in her way? With pleasure! A short man with a calico bandanna worn like a mask tried to grab her as she emerged from the alleyway, and Canna let him have it dead-center in the chest. He stumbled backward, a dark stain blossoming on his shirt. She kept right on going.

Rough ground and sharp rocks tore at her feet, but she didn't let it stop or even slow her. Past buildings and houses—the church *was* on fire, but the brief glimpse she had of the mutilated horror within almost made her glad of the fact; what manner of monster would *do* such a thing? Preacher Gaines hadn't been her favorite person in the world, not by far, but even he didn't deserve . . .

As she rounded the corner of the saloon, another figure suddenly appeared in her path. The dark shadow of a man, in sombrero and serape, twin pistols in hand . . . but it was what she could see of his face that made Canna cry out.

His face . . . his *eyes* . . . where his eyes should have *been* . . . gnarled knots of scar tissue twisting from temple to temple . . . the bridge of his nose a craggy ruin . . .

She brought up the gun to fire, but the man with no eyes fired first.

2

WHAT KIND OF MAN

AS HORSECOCK HAD told Nate, the homesteader couple—Walter, and Maggie, the missus—hadn't turned out to be his sort, no, not at all. Walter had been willing to undergo any amount of humiliation, degradation, abuse and pain to protect his wife and spare her from harm. Regardless of what it meant for himself.

Right decent of him. Noble. Good and proper. A worthy husband. A real man.

This lawyer-fellow, on the other hand . . .

Oh, this lawyer-fellow, this Emmerson Pryce, proved *exactly* the sort Horsecock was looking for. All arrogance and bluster. Proud. Haughty. Pompous as the day was long. *How-dare-you* this and *if-you-had-any-idea* that. Thinking himself better than anyone else on account of his wealth and his breeding and his education. His lofty station. His position in society. As if the likes of Horsecock weren't fit to shine his shoes.

Big-shot big talk, hot shit on a silver platter,

making demands, promising dire imprecations. The very *notion* of Horsecock coming into his house! The very *nerve*! Like he could drive Horsecock out with nothing more than his words and his ire, drive him out like a skulking stray dog with tail 'tween his legs.

It didn't last much beyond the first hit. And the first hit hadn't even been a hard one. Only a cuff upside the head to gain the lawyer's attention. Could hardly be the only time anyone had ever taken a swing at the puffed-up blow-hard, though his affronted reaction sure made it seem so.

For that, Horsecock had delivered the second hit, one with feeling. A lip-splitter, knocking Pryce onto his ass. The affrontedness vanished, replaced by a stark, dawning fear.

Guess what, even a big-shot hot-shit lawyer could be hurt. Important political connections didn't stop Horsecock's third hit from blacking an eye. A degree from some fancy college back East didn't prevent the fourth hit from loosening some teeth.

The third and fourth hits came later, though. The first two were sufficient to stop his *who-do-you-think-you-are* bluster, if not quite immediately reduce him to a sniveling, pleading, apologetic jelly. Enough to get him into a chair, lashed and secured, so's they could conversate.

The missus, well, she was meek as a mouse, not a fiber of fight or resistance in her. The spark had long since been snuffed from her spirit; Horsecock could see that plain as anything. It hung around her in a shawl of beaten-down acceptance.

Infuriated him, it did. She might've been a lively, vibrant lady once. Might've been sweet, and gentle.

With a pretty laugh, and a way of taking joy in such simple little things . . . a sprig of posies . . . a picnic . . . watching the sunset.

Been a long time since she'd laughed, or taken joy in much of anything. Although clearly frightened by the situation, something about the weary set of her posture suggested this was only another bad hand dealt in life's continuous card game.

Horsecock had employed his usual tactics, found them sound asleep, and rousted them with rough, sudden violence. Their place was finely furnished, and pin-neat. Not a speck of dust anywhere. Floors so clean, they could be et off of. With nary a maid or hired girl in evidence. All her own work, he felt certain.

And what thanks did she get?

Scant-fucking-little, was his guess.

There was, he soon ascertained, a kid . . . a boy, upstairs. Only then had the missus shown more than a flicker. "Please," she'd said, so breathy and timid, unable to meet Horsecock's eyes. "Our son, please don't hurt him; he's a deep sleeper, he won't—"

"Silence, woman!" the lawyer had interrupted, regaining some bluster like her temerity offended him; who'd given *her* leave to talk?!

Well, that was when Horsecock had blacked his eye. Then assured the missus he had no quarrel with the kid, so long as the kid didn't wake or intervene or try anything foolish. "Though, could be," he'd added, "there's some lessons here he'd do well to learn. Lessons about what kind of man his father is."

The kind who, unsurprisingly, proved none too eager to divulge the whereabouts of his money, even when certain indignities were suggested against the person of his wife. Indignities which Horsecock, as was his wont, laid out in graphic detail.

Soon, he was well and truly riled-up again, straining at his trouser-buttons and rarin' to go. The missus had gone the drear color of wash-water. Not sobbing, not begging. Just resigned to her sorry fate. Hopeless. Broken. The lawyer's expression seethed a craven, hateful, impotent fury.

"Do what you want," he spat. "You will anyway. Not as if I have a choice!"

"Wellnow, Mr. Pryce, sir, I'm surprised. A smart, educated fella such as yourself ought to know there's always a choice."

Just then, though, somewhere outside, the night's quiet went rudely interrupted with gunshots, screams, and raised voices.

"Damnation," Horsecock said. "Don't it just figure? Right when we're reachin' the fun part. But, no, y'know what? Nate and them can handle their own hoo-raw. We still got unfinished business."

Again in graphic detail, as was his wont, he laid out the lawyer's choices for him . . . though he already had a fair certainty of what the answers would be. So, too, judging by the look of her, did the missus. A man such as this? Endure violating indignities hisownself? Sacrifice a finger or three? Just to spare *her* the suffering?

To make absolute sure, Horsecock unlimbered his namesake from confinement and worked a curled fist up and down its engorged, veiny thickness by way of emphasis. Her hopelessness, her brokenness, her sorry resignation. His spiteful, selfish, affronted offense.

"Now, there's a chance she might be all right, after," he said. "Moreso of a chance, though, I'd think, not. Slight-built woman, your missus. Likely to be somewhat the worse for wear. Or, sad but true, they can die of it, sometimes, I hear. Internal ruptures, they call it."

"Kill her, then, if you're going to! Split her wide open! Fuck the bitch inside-out for all I care!"

If *that* didn't make it absolute sure, nothing would. Even Horsecock, with his long history of conversations such as this, was taken aback by the ugliness, the venom. He paused mid-stroke and just looked at the man.

"She's your *wife*," he said. "Keeper of your *house;* I seen how nice it is, how clean. Mother of your *child*; gave you a son! From what I hear, a chunk of what you've got squirreled away come from *her* inheritance! And you'd . . . you'd sit right there and watch a brute like me go on and fuck her to death."

"What if I would? What's it to you?"

"Not much to me. Sommat more to *her*, I reckon. Aren't you supposed to be her husband? Love and protect her? Love and protect your family, putting them before anything? Before money? Before yourself? What kind of man don't do that? What kind of man *are* you?"

Outside, the noisy hoo-raw continued; he recognized Nate's voice in what sounded like negotiations and figured someone in town had kept their guns and their wits about them enough to force a stand-off. He also smelled smoke, probably Unholy Joe having torched another church after making his customary gory offering to the Devil.

All of that, though, was a notice-in-passing. His full attention stayed fixed on the lawyer before him. Who had, somehow, dug through his fear and found his poisonous nature.

"You come into *my* house—!" Pryce's face was florid, nostrils flared. Spittle flew from his split lip.

"Right." Horsecock swung a leg, struck the chair, sent it crashing sideways with the lawyer still bound to it. The rest of Pryce's tirade was lost in a pained grunt. He lay there, groaning, as Horsecock stuffed himself back into his trousers, buttoned up, and stood over him. "Don't need to hear the rest. *Your* house, how *dare* I, so on and so on."

He swung his leg again, this time driving the toe of his boot into Pryce's ribs. Something cracked, which pleased him. The lawyer bleated like a hurt goat, which pleased him more. Levering the chair upright, he administered another backhanded clout. Pryce lolled, dazed, clinging to consciousness by a fraying thread.

"You sit tight and hold your tongue," he said. "Need to have me a few words with your missus."

Through all of this, she'd only stayed as she was: wash-water dreary, resigned, hopeless, accepting. He'd tied her to a chair as well, though probably hadn't even needed to. There she sat, head down, simply waiting for whatever bad cards life would *next* turn from the deck.

"Ma'am? Missus?"

"Please, don't hurt my boy," she breathed. "Don't hurt my Emmett. He's a sound sleeper. He won't cause any trouble. He's a good boy. Please, let him be."

Horsecock cast a glance ceilingward. Some sound sleeper, indeed . . . between this and whatever was going on outside, damn well *have* to be . . . or, he was up there, terrified and awake, huddled under the blankets trying to wish all the awfulness away.

Which, another boy, the long-ago Horace Cochran, could have told him, wouldn't work. Not by wishing, not by praying. Not by nothing. Some awfulness, well, some awfulness had itself a way of lingering.

"Tell me 'bout this inheritance you come into," he said.

"A . . . a great-uncle, I hardly knew him. Oil money. Thirty thousand."

He whistled. "That *is* a tidy sum. Your husband there, he took charge of it?"

"Yes. Yes, of course."

"Of course."

Pryce stirred himself enough to mumble another don't-you-dare, this one directed at his wife. Barely sparing him a glance, Horsecock kicked him again, knocking him out cold solid.

"He got it locked up in that safe?" Horsecock asked.

She nodded dully. "And our own savings."

"You know the combination, don't you? He lets you, because his thumb's on you so good, he'd never expect you to go against him."

Her head bowed in admission.

"Bet you've thought about it a time or two," he went on. "Taking the money, taking your boy, catching a fast stage to the nearest train station."

"I . . . I couldn't . . . " she said. "He's my husband."

"You seen pretty clear here tonight what kind of a husband he is. What kind of a man he is. Though, somehow, I reckon it weren't no surprise."

"No." She said it flat, without emotion. "No surprise at all."

"That the kind of man you want your boy to grow up like? Grow up admirin'?"

Her gaze flew to his, showing real feeling for the first time. "Emmett is nothing like his father! He—" She bit off the rest.

"Hates him?" Horsecock provided. "Is afeared of him? He use his hands on the boy, too? Oh, now, no need to lie to me, missus. I seen your bruises."

A haggard little sob escaped her, not that he needed further confirmation. He turned and cast an eye at Mr. Emmerson Pryce, insensate on the floor. No movement from him. Nor from upstairs, the kid presumably well-trained to lay low and keep quiet.

Meanwhile, whatever was going on outside seemed to have taken some wild turns; sounded like a full-on battle was raging. Had a detachment from Fort Winston happened to ride in late-arrival and unannounced? A posse on the trail of the Nasty Bastards catching up at an inconvenient moment? One of the ranchers whose property they'd not yet gotten to having armed and rallied his men to ride?

Well, he'd deal with all that soon enough. Right now, he had unfinished business in this room.

"You don't even care so much about the money," he said to the missus. "You'd tell me the combination, if you weren't more worried about what he'd do to you after."

"He'd be furious," she said. Putting it some mildly,

maybe; the knowledge her husband wouldn't just beat her but likely beat her to *death* hung heavy between them.

"Here's the thing . . . " Horsecock gestured at the window. "My boss, he'll be none too pleased I leave this house empty-handed. But . . . " He drew his gun. "We c'n both come out ahead, if'n you say the word."

She looked at him, the confusion in her eyes becoming understanding, then disbelief, and then . . . there it was . . . the tiniest budding of actual hope. A possible light at the end of a long, dismal tunnel. Freedom. A future. A chance.

"You'd . . . "

"Be our secret," he said. "No one else need ever know, not even your boy. People can be real sympathetic. Such a loss, such an ordeal. They'd hardly have cause for suspicion or fault-findin', would they? But I have to hear it from you."

"Yes," she whispered. She blinked, as if at her own audacity. Then, she met his eyes, and repeated it stronger. "Yes. Please."

He'd been pretty sure she wouldn't disappoint him. But, you never could tell. Did his heart good to hear the resolve in her tone.

Better yet, Mr. Pryce had revived some, regaining sufficient coherence to realize what had happened and what was happening. To have heard some of their exchange. To know who had signed the warrant . . . who would have the last laugh.

The expression on his face!

Perfection.

Before Pryce could ruin it by spouting some bullying bluster, Horsecock put a bullet through his head.

The missus—the widow—jumped a bit in her bonds. That was all. She stared at the corpse, skull like a broken crockery pot leaking stew onto the nice bedroom rug. Body settling, the way they did. Deflating, almost. Already appearing diminished, so less big and imposing, so less a presence looming huge, overshadowing, controlling her life. No longer a domineering force of nature. Just a cooling lump of dead meat.

Horsecock gave her several seconds to take in the scene before gently reminding her about the combination. Absently, still staring, she recited off numbers. They worked fine and dandy. He opened the safe, letting out another whistle at the sight of neatly-bundled stacks of bills and a pile of small drawstring bags.

After loading his loot-sack, he went around behind her chair. "Going to cut partway through the ropes," he told her, as he'd told Walter and Maggie at their homestead. "A while and some effort, you'll get yourself loose. I'll be long gone by then."

Long gone, and fully satisfied, more satisfied than he'd been in a right damn long time.

Rounding in front of her again, he set a couple of the bundled bill-stacks and drawstring coin-bags in her lap. She glanced from them to him, puzzled. "What . . . ?"

"Tell folks it was hid elsewheres, or sommat, not in the safe," he said. "Ain't much, but it'll do you and your boy a fresh start. Take good care of him, now, y'hear?"

"I will." A tear escaped her eye, the kind of tear he

liked best of all. "Thank you."

He bent to bestow a chaste, tender kiss on her forehead. "Ma'am."

Then he shouldered his loot-sack and went to find out what kind of trouble Nate and the Nasty Bastards had gotten themselves into now.

3

So Many Questions

SHE'D SEEN DEAD people before, Mina had. It was an inevitability, even for a girl her age. Life was hard, especial' in the west. Grandparents took poorly. Tiny little babies failed to thrive. Accidents happened to anyone, man, woman, or child. See dead people? Sure, she had. Sure.

But . . . usually when they were laid out for the viewing, neat-clothed and hair-combed. Tucked neat into a casket, face serene, eyes closed, hands folded. So's that neighbors could pass by and pay their final respects before the lid got nailed on once and for all . . . then it was into the ground, into the rectangular hole. Dirt shoveled over. A cross or marker set up.

Before then, though? Before the undertaker and gravediggers were summoned to ply their trades? No, never. Until tonight.

Until tonight, when they'd found Ol' Man Starkey torn all to pieces. Stinking of the slaughter. Parts of him strewn. Parts of him savaged and gnawed and eaten. The blood-puddle, thick and slick, clammy.

Seeing someone honest-to-gosh *die*? Right in front of her?

Honest-to-gosh *killed*? Full on *murdered*?

No, that either, she never had seen, not once. Again, until tonight. When the bad man with the bow put an arrow through the poor Truther-boy's back, pinning him to the dog-yard fence the way a butterfly might get pinned to a cork-board. The way his hands and feet rattled fitful at the planks . . . the way he gurgled his last . . . then just went so limp. And him just a kid, just a kid same as her.

Leegam, his name had been. Or so Mina thought, at least, given how Saleel had shrieked it.

What about the shaggy-coat Emmett had thrown her lantern at? Set him blazing afire in a horrible, howling, flailing dance? Did that count? They'd gone on running, hadn't waited to watch, hadn't actually *seen* him fall and die. Die he had, though, according to his vengeful brother, who'd meant so to have his pound-of-flesh payback.

She decided the burned shaggy-coat didn't full count. Then she wondered why in the world she was fretting over which ones counted and which ones didn't.

Two of the other shaggy-coats most certainly *did* count. She'd seen plenty when **Man-Mountain** reared up behind them in the tall grass, bigger and broader than them both put together. Seized them a head in each hand, he had, and dashed their skulls together so hard they broke like shell-boiled eggs.

Dex, the bad man with the bow? Who would've killed Emmett next, if **Deadly Lotus** hadn't sliced his arrow clean through in mid-flight? Did he count too? Or had he still been alive, buried beneath a pecking mass of beaks and black feathers, when she and Emmett got scooped up and spirited away?

Wasn't a flock of crows for-real called a murder?

Maybe she'd ask **Princess Crow-Feather**, if she had the chance. She had so many questions. So very, very many. Some, much more important than others.

Such as, was she going to see anyone else die? Her friends? Her own brother? They all were hurt, and she didn't know how bad. She remembered Albert with the side of his face bloody, his ear cut to ribbons. Albert telling Emmett to take her and run like blazes, and Emmett doing so even as Mina pleaded with Cody to wake up. Where skinny Emmett found the strength, she couldn't guess, what with her struggling every step of the way too.

Then Dex had shot Emmett in the leg, and he and Mina'd gone sprawling, and the next arrow would've been Emmett's end if not for their unexpected rescue.

The men who'd done the scooping and spiriting were rough but ordinary, carnival roustabouts. Armed with hatchets and sledgehammers rather than guns, they'd appeared at a signal from **Deadly Lotus** before the swordswoman raced on toward the house. Two went to Emmett, who had gone dreadful still. A third went to the smaller Truther-boy, the one with the freckles, whose name Mina didn't know; he was crying silently, rubbing at his throat where Dex had lifted him. There was blood at his mouth too, which scared her a moment, until she remembered he'd bit one of the shaggy-coat men.

A fourth carnie came to Mina. He had whiskey

breath and a scruffy, disreputable look, but just then he might've been a parade-dressed cavalry soldier far as she was concerned. "It's all right," he told her. "We've got you. It's all right."

"Cody," she said. "My brother. And Albert. And Saleel. They're—"

"It's all right," he repeated. "We'll bring you all back to camp. You'll be safe there."

Somehow, with a brisk efficiency she'd barely noticed, the men had rigged a litter for Emmett, hoisted her and the Truther-boy onto a sturdy pony, and were already leading them away from Starkey's place. She craned to look for Cody and the others, but couldn't see much. As she opened her mouth to ask some of her many questions, she burst into a fresh spate of sobbing and tears instead. The freckled Truther-boy, riding behind her, patted her awkwardly on the shoulder.

She must've swooned into a daze, because in what seemed no time at all, they were amid the colorful tents and wagons, surrounded by carnival folk. Whole camp was awake, lanterns lit, fires blazing. There were kind words, and blankets, and wet cloths to wipe the worst of the bloodstains. There were ladles of cool water and mugs of strong-brewed tea. There was a little dog, yipping anxiously, hopping as if on springs, trying to sniff everybody.

"He won't bite," someone said, in a youthful, gentle voice. The black-braided girl they'd seen before picked up the dog, tapped its snub nose, and fixed it with a calm gaze. The dog quieted at once, whining, wiggling its hind end in a stifled attempt to wag its stubby tail.

"You . . . you're her, ain't you?" Mina found her

wits enough to finally form a question. "**Princess Crow-Feather.** Those were your birds, right?"

"My friends. They speak to me, listen to me, let me see through their eyes. You may call me Jane, if you like. What is your name?"

Up close, she didn't seem entirely an Injun . . . a half-breed, maybe? And probably not a real princess. Either way, Mina reckoned it'd be rude to ask.

"Mina. Mina McCall. I, uh, don't know his. But the other boy's . . . where is he? Where's Emmett?"

"They took him for the healing."

"The healing? The doctor? **Doctor Oddico**?"

Jane smiled. "Oh, he is no surgeon or sawbones," she said.

But, before she could elaborate or Mina inquire further, a second group of roustabouts returned to the campground. Cody was with them, woozy but upright, stubborn as ever and no doubt insisting he was fine to walk. Albert, head swathed in bandages, rode one of the ponies. Two of the men bore a litter, upon which lay a sheet-draped body. Saleel kept pace beside it, holding poor Leegam's dead hand.

"Cody!" Mina shed the blanket someone had put around her, up and off like a shot. She near knocked him off his feet, hugging him tight-tight-*tight* as he staggered.

"Am I *ever* glad to see you," he said, hugging her tight-tight-*tight* in return.

"It's them, we were wrong, we were wrong, they ain't wicked at all. They rescued us! Fought the bad men! They're helping! They—"

"I know."

The Truther-boy rushed past them to embrace

Saleel. Another hustle-bustle of carnie folk ensued, a lot of conversations going on simultaneous. The gist of it seemed to be that they were on alert for further trouble. Men were on watch, men who had guns in addition to hatchets and hammers.

"Emmett?" Cody asked, after a worried glance around.

"Something about a healing," Mina said. "How hurt are you?"

"Just a bump."

"Don't you lie to me, Cody Cornelius McCall."

"One sore damn *hell* of a bump." Wincing, he pressed fingertips to his head, and admitted, "Might've cracked my noggin. Aches fit t' split. Everythin' keeps spinnin'. Feels like I'm gonna spew up my supper."

"After what we all seen tonight, who wouldn't?"

"Worse'n just that."

"Come on, then, you lummox, and sit y'self down!" As she took over fussing the way their mother would've done, she added, "This here's Jane, **Princess Crow-Feather.** Sicced her bird-friends on Dex, saved Emmett's life."

It occurred to her briefly she hadn't seen any of the other star performers. **Man-Mountain** and **Deadly Lotus** had not returned with the others, nor was there any sign of the **Living Ghost, Blind Bandito, Mother Sybil,** or **Tom Short, the World's Smallest Negro.** Or any immense beasts with jaws like giant ivory bear-traps, such as what they'd seen in the tent. Or even **Doctor Oddico,** who apparently wasn't a surgeon or sawbones, whatever that might mean.

The fancy-man who'd come to town, though, was

in obvious attendance, taking charge and giving orders. He persuaded Saleel to part with Leegam's body and let it be taken into one of the wagons for safe-keeping. The Truther-girl then huddled near to one of the fires, holding onto a mug of tea as if more for the warmth than anything else. Her wide, dark eyes looked wider and darker than ever, deep and hollow as caverns. Blaming herself, Mina guessed, for having brung the boys on this moonlit adventure, only to end up getting one of them killed.

Two more roustabouts arrived with a mule and a cart—Ol' Man Starkey's mule and cart? Must've been; they hadn't been in the barn, only the house and the kennel—laden with more bodies. Treated with far less respect than Leegam's was, Mina noted. Piled in all unceremonious, a mound of blood-matted shaggy coats . . .

And, atop them, a hideous raw and red flayed skeletal thing she barely recognized as Dex, the bad man with the bow. The birds had done *that*? She turned an eye half-awed and half-uneasy on **Princess Crow-Feather**, it suddenly being hard to think of her as anything so prosaic as 'Jane.'

Cody kept on trying to refuse further attention, though when he drank a cupful of water, he of a sudden bent double and spewed up his supper after all, then came over so shaky Mina decided she'd brook no further stoic foolishness on his part. At her urging, the fancy-man ushered her brother along to the same large tent where Albert's litter had been carried.

As well as, it turned out, the one bearing Emmett, because there he was. Up on a table instead, bright-lit by lanterns. His pantleg had been cut away in wide flaps, baring his thigh with the gory arrowhead protruding and a tourniquet cinched above the blood-seeping wound. The feathered end must've been snapped off at the back of his leg to let him lie flat. From here, she couldn't tell if he were even breathing.

Three figures surrounded him, and despite the harsh lighting, it could've been a scene from one of those Shakespeare plays their ma talked about.

To be fair, only one of them *looked* like a proper witch, **Mother Sybil** with her gnarled knuckles and long grey straggles of hair. In her shapeless sack-dress, shawl wrapped around her, yes, she looked like a proper witch indeed.

But the **Living Ghost**, his red hood down, red kidskin gloves off to reveal eerily elegant and beautiful hands as pure white as the rest of him, *could* have passed for a male witch . . . there *were* male witches, weren't there? Warlocks?

As for the third, standing squatly bow-legged on a stool pulled up beside the table . . . didn't witches also have imps? The Devil's familiars? Small, dark and hunched? All malformed and misshapen?

Then, no, she saw it wasn't an imp at all, but **Tom Short**. Who, at less than two feet tall, indeed could have been **The World's Smallest Negro**. He had an overlarge, lumpy head set askew on a bent neck, a heavy brow, and his skin was darker even than their pa took his coffee.

When he spoke, it was in the same deep cannon-volley that had boomed at them so much earlier in the evening, calling them townie cow-splats and telling them there were no free shows. Even now, when he wasn't booming, it carried in such a rumble Mina felt it in her bones.

"Gonna have to pull it soon or never," he said. "You best be ready."

"I am," said the **Living Ghost.** His voice, same as his hands and alabaster features, possessed an eerie, elegant beauty. If the full moon could talk, Mina thought, that was what it would sound like. Cool, remote, silvery.

Mother Sybil, who turned to them as they came in, sounded less like a cackling crone of a witch than she did someone's dear granny, altogether at odds with her appearance. "Stay back a bit, children. Try not to be frightened. We mean him no harm."

"Over here," said the fancy-man, Sebastian Farstairs. "We'll be out of the way, and your brother can sit before he falls over." He guided them to another portion of the tent, near where Albert's litter had been placed upon another table.

Cody didn't so much as protest. It was bad, then. Dire bad. He'd gone all sallow, shakier than ever. As soon as he reached a bench, he sank onto it and lowered his head to his knees.

Mina glanced in Albert's direction. More carnies—an elderly man with poofs of dandelion-fuzz hair, and a plump lady whose creamy-pink skin was covered in tattoos—had undone the bandages around his head to wash the crusted mess of whatever remained of his ear. Albert himself moaned awful piteous, trying to twist away from their ministrations. The tattooed lady held a green glass bottle to his lips.

"Drink it on down, laddie-o," she said in a trilling lilt. "Drink it on down. T'will null the pain."

Albert did drink, screwing his mouth to a grimace

at some medicinal foulness. He shuddered, then blinked. Catching sight of Mina, he asked, as Cody had done, "Emmett?"

She pointed. "They're . . . helping him, I think . . . "

"They are," said the elderly man. Behind nose-pinch spectacles, his eyes were as green as the fancy-man's, though bright more with concern than charming twinkles. "Our ways might seem strange to you, what you're about to see. But I give you my promise, the promise of **Doctor Oddico**, they truly do mean him no harm. We none of us mean any of you *any* harm."

Fretful though she was about Cody, Mina went on her tip-toes to watch. **Mother Sybil** held Emmett's leg at hip and knee, immobilizing it. The **Living Ghost** pushed his robe's sleeves well up his snow-white arms.

"Now," rumbled **Tom Short.** "Pulling it . . . now!"

Mina flinched, expecting him to grab the arrowhead and give it a hard yank. Instead, his heavy brow furrowed into deep creases, fists clenched at his own sides. A brief but powerful shockwave, as if from a silent explosion, made her ears pop.

And the gory, broken arrow, untouched, shot straight up several inches into the air. It hung there a moment, dripping, then flung itself to the straw- and sawdust-strewn floor.

Her chin about bounced off her toes. Had she really just seen . . . ? No, it couldn't have been . . .

Blood spouted afresh from Emmett's leg, a regular geyser of it. Had to be a good sign, had to mean at least he weren't yet dead, but gosh-*sakes* so much blood!

Quick as a flash, the **Living Ghost** clasped his

pale hands to the wound, re-gloving them again in vivid crimson. He threw his head back in a carved-statue rictus of suffering. It put Mina in mind of pictures from Italian cathedrals. The whitest white marble, exquisite detail.

The blood no longer spouting, it pooled on the table and ran in rivulets . . . but it was slowing. It was slowing. Because Emmett had died? Was that why?

Then Emmett gasped and bucked, his eyes flying open. He stared up at the people gathered over him— what a scene it must have been, from his view!—and tried to struggle, but they still held him firm.

"Easy, there," **Tom Short** told him. "Easy, now."

"Emmett!" Mina called. "It's all right! We're safe!"

"M-Mina?"

"Let them help you!"

Releasing a shuddering sigh, the **Living Ghost** lifted his newly reddened hands from Emmett's leg. No fresh blood spouted, or even flowed. The wound, mess though it was, looked . . . closed.

Her chin could have bounced off her toes yet again. She turned to Cody, but he still had his head cradled low to his knees and hadn't been looking!

She turned to **Princess Crow-Feather** next, who nodded solemnly and said, "The healing."

"Magic?" asked Mina, but the other girl only shrugged.

"As fair a word as any," Mr. Farstairs said. "Not a magic *trick*, don't take that idea." He grinned, flicked his fingers, and produced a playing card—the ace of diamonds—from nowhere. "We have those, too, of course. But this . . . this is different."

"Huh?" Cody blearily attempted to raise his head.

THE NIGHT SILVER RIVER RUN RED

"You missed it, you lummox! You missed the whole gol-durned thing! No one will ever believe it—"

"*He* will," said **Princess Crow-Feather**, indicating Emmett.

Who, by then, was sitting up, gingerly prodding at his leg in genuine amazement. Mina hurried closer for a better look as **Mother Sybil** laved away the worst of the blood. The wound *had* closed, into a pink and pulpy tenderness maybe, but it *had* closed! Was like something healed up a week or so out!

There'd be scars of a certain, scars for the rest of his life. He might have a limp ever after, like her and Cody's pa. But he would live! He'd not lose his leg!

Magic, she'd said? Forget magic; a *miracle*!

To think, she'd been full-to-brimming of questions *before*!

4

More Scenes from a Massacre

THE WOMAN WAS going to fire, going to shoot him, but he fired first.

Once. Once was all it took. Once was all it ever took.

Shot the gun from her grasp.

It likely hurt her, and for that he was sorry. Still, had to be done.

As she stifled a cry, springing backward, shaking her pained hand, he twirled both of his own guns so their trigger-guards looped his thumbs. He raised his arms, elbows bent, palms toward her, fingers splayed. A gesture of non-hostility. A gesture only; the merest flick of his wrists would bring both weapons instantly ready.

"Peace, *Senora*," he said. "I am on your side."

"You . . . how . . . who . . . " she stammered. He sensed her sharp scrutiny, heard the uncertain shift of her posture. Could almost pluck her thoughts from the air, like the clicking of telegraph code.

"Yes," he said. "I am with the carnival. My name

is Felipe. There is no time. They are coming. You are alone?"

"My husband . . . the post office . . . but your eyes . . . "

"Never mind that. There is no time."

The drumming of footsteps, many pairs of boots running in several directions. Voices. Shouting and swearing. Gunshots.

Sweat, gunpowder, whiskey, tobacco, piss, shit, blood, and death.

The muffled sobbing of terrified, cloth-gagged little girls.

The crackle of hungry flames, the groan of burned and weakening timbers, the smell of smoke, a basking heat.

Heartbeats. Fast with fear, fast with anger, fast with excitement.

Someone rounded the corner of the building—a saloon—at a rapid pace, reloading. Felipe spun in a smooth and fluid motion that put him between the woman and the newcomer. The outlaw. Armed and dangerous. Hell-bent on murder.

One shot. One less heartbeat.

Two others popped up from behind a wagon, popped up like targets at a mechanized gallery.

Two more shots. Throat. Head. Two more down.

The woman, convinced. At his back. Following without hesitation.

Horses in a panic, rearing and kicking, whinnying in their stalls.

High overhead, the midnight pull of the moon, round and full. A presence felt even when unseen. Further on, piercing in their silence, cold dispassionate stars.

Footsteps, but . . . above? Slow, soft-treading, deliberately placed. On the roofline of what could only be a bakery. Trying to get into position to have a clear angle on the post office, Felipe reasoned after consulting an intuitive inner map of the town's layout.

The rifleman—the tang of a well-oiled long blued steel barrel was unmistakable—had an eagerness about him. Young and gutsy, clever enough to be cautious but too thrilled to be scared. Didn't think for a second anything could happen to him. His breathing was rapid, through the nose. One of his nostrils made the faintest whistle on each inhalation.

More than enough.

Had this been in a performance, to impress the paying audience, Felipe would've gone for a trick-shot. A toss-spin-catch-shoot, or a ricochet, or something equally showy.

But this wasn't a performance.

The rifleman's nose whistled again. For the very last time. A moment later, his body tumbled off the roof to lay dead and spreadeagled in Silver River's main street.

Plans were nice and all, but sooner or later, more often than not, they'd go from fine to fucked-right-up with little damn warning.

With this plan, they'd even *had* some damn warning. Should have *known* Pete's blather about boom-town riches was too good to be true. Easy money. Uh-huh.

"Easy money, my ass," Sue muttered.

As if it hadn't gone fucked-up enough at the mercantile. At least they'd come out of that one with some hefty cash, and they'd been able to rid themselves of whiny Pete. Even better, despite the fool's noisy attack on his spinster auntie, it hadn't been what alerted the town. Whatever else happened, she, Leonard, Billy-Jack, and Otto wouldn't be facing the blame.

Who'd gone to the livery? Shilo and Jessie? No, they'd been with Tubber. Didn't much matter now, anyway. The fucked-uppedness had arrived.

She, for one, was glad. There was something to be said for doing the job quiet-like, and she didn't need her any sick games like Gus and Bertrand, and she harbored no particular crusade like Unholy Joe ... but, quiet-like got boring after a while. Her trusty Johnny Thunder didn't care for being kept on the hush.

It'd been, therefore, a bit of a relief when the shots and screams started, and Nate hollered they might as well cut on loose.

She'd gone straight out the front doors of the mercantile, spied a man in a ridiculous striped nightshirt trying to shimmy down a drainpipe from a third-floor window—the nightshirt had got all bunched to his waist, giving the world far more of a view of his pasty backside than was needed—and let Johnny Thunder do what Johnny Thunder did best.

A few other townsfolk who must've been hiding in hopes of waiting it out unnoticed had a change of mind and made breaks for it; they didn't get far. Sue took a great personal delight in blowing the tits off some sour-faced bitch who reminded her of every 'decent' lady that used to scold her to sit nice and speak mild and act like a good girl.

Over by the livery, half a dozen darkies in a mighty pissed-off mood had caught themselves somebody or three to bludgeon with hayrakes, while a distraught black mammy caterwauled up a storm. Until, that was, more Nasty Bastards closed in, forcing a darkie retreat.

The church was in flames, Unholy Joe capering around it while chanting to the Devil and stump-humping the neck hole of the preacher's severed head, or whatever the hell that sick fuck got up to. Sue spied that other sick fuck Horsecock's mare, Blondie, by a tree in someone's yard . . . but didn't spy Horsecock himself.

Nor was there any sign yet of Dex and them, though with the moon so high they should've met back up with the main gang by then. Hardly her problem, though. Nate could deal with—

Except Nate suddenly had himself a post office problem to deal with. A sureshot of a problem, at that. A sureshot with company; she knew a fellow shotgun when she heard one. Instead of their casualties being only a couple men got the better of at the livery, they were down another eight or nine in the span of mere minutes.

Eight or nine! An actual damn body-count! Jessie included, was Sue's guess; she'd heard a woman shrieking after one of those roaring blasts, sounding some familiar. 'Sides, it were just them two females in the gang, her and Jessie. Nasty Bastardettes, as some had liked to wisecrack, until Jessie threatened to turn their nutsacks into coin-purses. The thought of Jessie dead—which likely meant Shilo as well—seemed impossible.

Then, even *Nate* took a bullet, which was when the fucked-uppedness officially reached a state of much-too-damn-far. Shot wasn't fatal, or *immediately* so anyways, but it threw everything all a'tizzy.

Leonard had to step in, yelling for someone to set fire to the goddamn post office already, burn the cocksuckers out. When Billy-Jack tried, hucking a blazing torch through a window, well, slap-your-face if the sureshot cocksucker in there didn't shoot the *torch*, extinguishing it mid-fucking-*air*!

And *then*, shit-for-breakfast, some *other* gunslinger invited himself to the party! Bang-bang-bang, adding to the body count! One of the newer recruits, a piss-and-vinegar kid hoping to make a name and win favor, got picked off a rooftop as neat as you please.

"Forget the cocksucking post office!" Sue hollered. "Time t' cut our losses and get the hell gone!"

He'd crept into the house—the shack, to be honest; drunk as he was he still knew it was a shack, as wrecked and wretched as Milo Dunnings himself—without waking any of them.

A sign, he s'posed. A sign he were doing the right thing. The only right thing, mayhap, he'd ever done for his family. See them off quick, by a loving hand. Rather than wait for Death's dark angels to come to their door, the way they'd come for the rest of Silver River.

A fat tallow candle sputtered in a clay crock on the table. Letting it burn all night was an expense they could ill afford, and a hazard as well, but the lil'uns sometimes took frightened. And, if Daisy had to get up to fetch her momma some water or medicine, it spared her having to strike a light.

His wife, so thin and frail, had three of the lil'uns sleeping all a'pile in the bed with her like baby barn-kittens. The bigger two of the lil'uns shared a cot, lying head-to-foot so's they could kick each other in the face.

Boys. He and his own brother had been that very way when they were young. Bicker and fight like nobody's business. But let anyone *else* try to mess with one of them? Oh, there'd be hell to pay, and a'plenty.

On another cot, wedged between the stove and the woodbox, was his Daisy. Such a good girl, she was. Always had been. Uncomplaining. Tireless. Looking after the lil'uns, looking after her momma. Doing her best to keep the place clean, the chores done, the rags they called clothes passably mended.

Twelve years old, and the weight of the world already on her. Even in slumber, worry-lines creased her brow, aging her beyond her years. As if her very dreams were filled with work and toil rather than happy scenes.

While he, her useless excuse for a pa, cared for little more than where his next bottle might come from.

"M'sorry, girl," he mumbled, tears dribbling down his stubbly cheeks. "M'sorry. Done d'served better, you did."

He drew his belt-knife. Metal scraped some on metal, leaving the sheath. It looked dull and rusty. He hoped it was sharp enough for the job. Hadn't had it to the whetstone in . . . couldn't remember.

His Daisy-girl crinkled her nose at his approach. Whiskey-breath? His general unwashed reek? If she woke, she'd give him that *look*, and Milo didn't think he could bear it.

Lordy, how his hands were a'shaking! He felt his will weaken and berated himself a shameful coward.

This one right thing! This one, last, only right thing!

Placing one shaking hand over her eyes—so's to not have to see that *look*, just in case she did wake—with the other he brought the blade's edge to her throat.

It . . . wasn't sharp. Wasn't very sharp at all.

He had to push hard. Had to saw, and lean his weight into it. Covering her eyes. Holding her head pressed firm to the cot. As blood bubbled like crude oil welling up from the ground . . . as her mouth gulped the way a landed fish's did . . . as she struck and scratched at his arms . . . as she struggled . . . as she stilled.

Milo sank to the floor beside her cot, quietly weeping. His girl, oh, his girl, his good Daisy-girl!

But, he'd done it. He'd done it, and the others would be easier.

Getting up, he moved to the bed where his wife

slept amid that kitten-pile of lil'uns. Barely skin-and-bones, she was. Hair brittle as straw. Couldn't more than sit up for an hour most days, let alone stand, or eat.

Doc Muldoon suspected it were a cancer in her, this time. A cancer, in growing where no more babies ever would. Nothing *he* could do about it, beyond giving her the laudanum, and even *that* had to be watered to make it stretch. A specialist, maybe, he'd said . . . not just from Winston City neither, but a big city, a real city.

She'd deserved better, too. All of them had. All of them, 'cept for him. He'd had far more better than he deserved, and squandered it. Selfish, thankless, and stupid.

As he drank in her beloved features as thirstily as he'd drink down a fresh bottle, gunfire started and screaming began.

Death's dark angels, their mission of silent slaughter all of a sudden turned into a wild midnight shoot-out!

It woke the lil'uns. It woke his wife.

And there he was, standing over her in the candlelight, the knife in his hand still dripping with their daughter's blood.

"Milo?" her wan, cracked lips whispered.

"M'sorry," he sobbed. "So g'damn sorry!"

Had he thought it would be easier? With her, and the lil'uns?

Like everything else in his life, he'd been wrong.

THE NIGHT SILVER RIVER RUN RED

This was *not* how Nate Bast had expected to die.

Hell, on some level, he'd expected *never* to die. Nasty Bastards never did.

If he *had* to, a blaze of glory would be better than hangin' . . . but, a lucky shot from some wiseass motherfuck holed up in a post office was hardly any damn blaze of glory.

He'd hitched himself as far back on the schoolhouse porch as he could go, leaning half-propped in a corner with his head tipped against the plank wall.

The pain—after the initial impact—wasn't so bad. Nor was the bleeding, at first. He'd had a moment's hope maybe the lucky shot motherfuck had only winged him. Then he'd got a good look. And now here he was with his own finger plugged into the hole in his chest to keep his breath from exiting the wrong way out his lung.

And what an unsettling sensation it was! The sucking, clasping tightness! Muscular convulsions and wet, biological heat! He'd had his fingers in plenty of orifices over the years, but . . .

As for the bleeding, he'd realized the only reason it didn't seem like much was because there wasn't much escaping external. Internal was another matter. Internal, he'd sprung one fuck of a leak.

He coughed. *That* hurt, that hurt a son-of-a-bitch. But the damp frogginess and the thick liquid mouthful he spat out was what disturbed him most. He was filling up inside. Like he was drowning.

Tubber, of all people, was the first one to reach him. Some-fucking-irony there; the degenerate babydrowner, shirt still soaked with bath-water.

"Boss," Tubber said. "Boss, aw shit."

"Aw shit indeed," Nate said. Talking hurt, too. "Motherfuck . . . holed my lung. We get his ass yet?"

From the ongoing sounds of the shouting and shooting, he wasn't surprised when Tubber shook his head. "No, boss, not yet. Shit. Look atcha. What can I do?"

"Night's taken a turn. They got reinforcements?"

"Some crazy Mexican; I don't rightly know."

Downstreet, Shotgun Sue was hollering something about cutting their losses and getting the hell gone. Nate didn't blame her. He was inclined to agree.

"Dex and . . . " The wrenching cough dragging up from his chest was the worst yet, a real dredger. Less like thick liquid spit, more like clotted vomit. Coating his throat, his nose, his chin. He gagged, and groaned.

"The Redwolf boys?" Tubber shook his head again. "Don't rightly know for them, neither, boss. We need to find you a doctor."

" . . . pretty sure . . . killed him already . . . "

No, he didn't want to die, even less wanted to die like this, on the porch of a fuckin' *schoolhouse* to boot . . .

. . . but all the doctors in the world wouldn't have made no damn difference as the relentless red tide rose up from within and drowned him in his own blood.

"All for You, oh great Master! Yea verily! These offerings of flesh and of fire, for You! In Your name, this scourge, this sacrifice!"

Beautiful, so beautiful, the burning church! The defilement of the priest!

And . . . what was this?

What was this his exalted gaze beheld?

Could it be?

Was it so?

Had he, finally, *finally*, succeeded? Been deemed worthy?

Josephiah rubbed at his smoke-stung eyes. He'd stripped, marked himself head to toe with profane symbols, twined the gutted preacher's intestines around his limbs and torso like garlands. His voice had gone hoarse from chanting. He ached, and he bled, and the mania was upon him, and . . .

Yes!

There!

Beyond the flames, coming nearer, looming larger!

A demon! A behemoth! Hell embodied!

A Way had been opened! At last! In this town of sin sowed and harvest-slaughtered, his prayers had been answered! His service would be rewarded!

Here was proof! No angels had stopped him, no God struck him down, and here was proof, proof incarnate, of who was stronger!

Laughing with joy, arms raised in supplication, he tottered forward, ready to fall to his knees and be abased at the feet of his Master's messenger. Let its diabolical piss shower upon him in scalding baptism . . . let him be so anointed!

Immense! Colossal!

Its very strides shook the earth!

Josephiah looked eagerly to see its cloven hooves stamping scorched craters, sought the sight of downcurved horns and fiery eyes. A scaled, lashing tail. The unfurling, leathery, smoldering splendor of wings.

He blinked, and rubbed more smoke from his eyes.

The cloven hooves were feet, huge feet but regular feet nonetheless. No horns, no tail, no splendid smoldering wings. In all, it looked very like a man. A large man, yes. Immense. Colossal. Bulging and rippling with muscle. But, a man.

Had . . . had it not yet fully assumed its demonic form?

Perhaps he'd presumed too much too soon. He prostrated himself before it.

"I await—" was as far as he got before everything ended with an ungodly crunch.

"Sue's right," Leonard said. "Nate's dead, and we'll all be right there with him if we don't get gone. Move!"

"What about—?" began Tubber.

"Ever'one else can look out for their own fuckin' selves!" Loyalty, far as he was concerned, only went so damn far. No profit to be gained by staying here, picked off one by one.

Call it a strategic withdrawal, call it a rout, call it an absolute fuckarow; made no nevermind to Leonard Loke if he lived through it. With some cash, ideally. The more the better, to sweeten stung pride.

The Night Silver River Run Red

They'd managed to regroup some—not the whole gang by any means, and probably not even half of them who'd made it into Silver River, but some—and when Leonard started barking orders because somebody goddamn had to, most of them fell in line as if glad to be told what to do. Helped he had two of his three regulars, Sue and Otto with him, though fuck knew where in this chaos Billy-Jack had gotten to after chucking that torch through the post office window.

Laying down suppressive fire, they broke cover and hauled ass. The majority of their horses had been left tethered in an orchard out the west side of town, but better to loop north and around rather than give the goddamn postmaster anymore easy targets.

"Still that crazy Mexican out there too," Tubber said.

"And where the hell's Horsecock?" Sue swiveled every whichway with Johnny Thunder. "Seen his mare not ten minutes ago—"

"Fuck Horsecock and fuck his fuckin' mare!"

Four shots snapped in quick succession. Four men went down, Otto among them. Leonard had the barest glimpse of a dark figure, there and then gone between buildings, serape flaring like a cape.

Tubber uttered a childish squeal, no doubt same as them babies made when he commenced with the dunkin', and split off to veer back the way they'd come. He ran with his hands over his head, the way a girl might fend off bats she feared would get in her hair. Made it 'bout twenty feet afore two shots cracked as one from two different directions. Both found their mark, spinning Tupper in a surprising-graceful pirouette of pinwheeling blood. He paused at the end for a moment, poised upright as if about to take a bow, then just collapsed.

"Show y'self, you chickenshit cunt!" Sue peppered with buckshot the front of the building behind which the serape had disappeared. "Dirty coward! Come out and fight fair!"

Leonard looked at her, incredulous. "Fight *fair*?"

"I don't have to make sense!" she screamed in his face.

Nothing seemed good to say to that, so he kept his mouth shut.

Half the rest of the group had also scattered, south toward the river or seeking places to hide. Some made it. Some didn't. Leonard stopped trying to keep track. He waved for Gus and Bertrand to take the lead, though apparently they interpreted it as to bolt like jackrabbits up the nearest alleyway.

"No, you . . . " Leonard hissed through his teeth. "Shit-a-goddamn. Sue! C'mon!"

He, Sue, and whoever else was left ran after them, gaining ground just in time to witness a woman in black spring from the shadows, lines of silver flashing arcs of moonlight.

One clean swipe, and son-of-a-bitch, there went Gus's head! Flipping up and over, while the rest of him kept on going a good couple-three strides. The woman, less than a split-second later, drove her other—*sword?* had to be!—into Bertrand, skewering him so that the tip poked out his back.

"Ain't we had enough?" Leonard heard himself yell to no one in particular. God, maybe, or the high-riding moon.

He stopped where he was, leveling his piece at the advancing woman. No way he'd be letting her within arm's reach! No way he'd bother with warnings, either. He fired. *That'd* do the—

Bullet met blade with a metallic zing. He saw the split chunks of lead fly apart at widening angles to either side of the woman's face, one grazing her exotic cheekbone, the other just missing her ear.

"The *fuck*!" he cried.

She smiled. Beautiful though she was, it wasn't a nice kind of smile. A slim eyebrow arched as if inviting him to try again.

"I goddamn got this!" Sue shoved Leonard aside, stepping forward and hefting Johnny Thunder. "See you pull that trick against a load of double-ought buck, you Chinee bitch!"

Turbulent darkness struck from above, engulfing Sue in a living tornado of crows. Their caws and shrieking obscured her screams, but couldn't obscure the shotgun's blast. Blown-to-bits bird-parts rained down. Feathers flew. Still, it made hardly a dint in the flock. Only served to incite the others.

Leonard backed away, unable to believe his eyes and unable *not* to. Now, in addition to the bird-parts, Sue's blood was raining down. Raining down as the crows pecked at her, tore at her. When he saw Johnny Thunder hit the red-muddied dirt, he knew it was over. She might still be alive in there, might still be screaming as they plucked flesh from bone, but it was over. Best he could do would be shoot her himself, make an end of it.

If he could *hit* anything in that death-cyclone!

And if, the cold for-profit voice in him added, he

could spare the ammunition. Didn't seem much point . . .

Backing away further, he bumped into something solid as an ox, broader than two bulls, and immovable. A glance up—and *up*!—showed him the biggest motherfucker he ever did see. A mountain of a man if ever there was one!

Arms like tree-trunks hooked around him, pinning his own arms at his sides, and *squeezed*. Leonard's elbows fractured inwards, ways they weren't made to bend. Ribs splintered into ivory toothpicks, all stabbing his gizzard.

So much for easy money.

Silver on silver, mirroring moonlight.

"Seventeen seconds . . . jolly good, old chap. Jolly . . . good. That's . . . a . . . new . . . record . . . "

Bertrand's hand fell, fingers loosely uncurling. His pocketwatch slipped from his grasp.

Tick-tock.

PART FOUR:

TOWARD THE DAWN

AFTER THE BURNING CHURCH crashed in upon itself, a hush once again blanketed the night. No more shots. No more screams. Only quiet.

Shane McCall waited as long as he could stand it, then hazarded a peek out the post office window. When no one took a shot at him, he cautiously emerged for a better look at the aftermath.

The carnage was . . . considerable. Corpses all up and down the thoroughfare, outlaws and his own friends and neighbors alike. He'd witnessed scenes some similar before, but this . . . this grieved him . . . this was the very definition of too close to home.

He wanted to call his wife's name, and dreaded doing so. If she didn't answer . . . if she hadn't made it . . .

And the kids! Cody, and Mina! Losing Canna would be bad. Losing them all would be unbearable. He'd never thought himself a family man until he'd become one, then couldn't imagine how he'd been anything else.

The church being set a ways apart had kept the fire from spreading. There was that consolation, at least.

Surely, there had to be *some* other survivors.

He limped to the center of the street, then caught movement from the corner of his eye and turned to see another man likewise there in the moonlight. They faced each other in a stance as natural and familiar as breathing. Both of them calm. Both of them steady. Arms held in loose curves, hands open at their sides. Fingers flexing.

This was it, then. This was how it would be. The timeless showdown. Whoever was quicker on the draw, him or this stranger—

"No!"

Something like a bedraggled ghost dashed between them, hair unbound and streaming, night-dress a tattered mess. She flung up one palm toward Shane, the other toward the man in the serape.

"No!" she repeated. "Don't! It's all right!"

"Canna . . . "

"Shane!"

He dropped his gun as she ran to him. Heedless of his stiff leg, he caught her when she leaped, swinging her around in an embrace, both of them laughing and crying and talking at once. When he set her down again, the other man had approached to a respectful distance. The rim of his sombrero cast a band of shadow across his face.

"*Senor*," the man said, giving a slight nod.

"You were the other gunslinger," Shane said. "You took out the one on the roof of the bakery. Hell of a shot!"

"I could say likewise of you."

"This is Felipe," Canna said. "He's with the carnival. They . . . they're all with the carnival."

Two other figures had joined them. Shane recognized the woman from a few days' previous, when she'd ridden in with the fancy-man to give away free passes to the show. Recognized, now as the pieces came together, Felipe and their giant companion as well. Not from having seen them before, but from their descriptions on the handbills posted all over town. Had put up one himself, in the post office window.

"We came to help," said Felipe. "These men, these killers, they meant to rob and murder."

"And worse," added the woman. "They were monsters. I regret we did not arrive sooner. Many more lives might have been spared. But we did not know."

Shane looked around as—tentatively, frightened, creeping like mice—the surviving citizens of Silver River began to gather. He saw most of the Scotts from the livery, Mayor Fritt's twin nieces holding onto each other as if never to let go, the wagonwright and his apprentice, the widow who took in washing. He saw harrowed faces and shock-glazed eyes.

He did *not* see his own children, and his heart sank in his chest. His arm tightened around Canna.

"But how *did* you know?" Canna asked.

A plaintive wail interrupted Felipe as he was about to answer. Moments later, a door banged open and Mrs. Pryce, the lawyer's wife, burst into view. Like the rest of them, she was in her night-clothes, and utter disarray. Tearful, with red welts encircling her wrists as if she'd had to struggle free from being tied, she ran to them.

"My boy!" she sobbed. "My Emmett! Oh, God! Someone, please, someone, help!"

"Is he . . . hurt?" Shane could barely bring himself to put forth even that much; he knew Emmett. A friend of Cody's. Scrawny kid, but a good one. A far better one than he might've been, considering his father.

"He's *gone*!" Mrs. Pryce wrung her hands. "I went to his room and his bed, it was *empty*! I thought he must be up there, keeping still, you know, as he does, when there's trouble, but—"

"Wait, *gone*?" Canna pulled away from Shane and took Mrs. Pryce by the upper arms. "As in, he snuck out? Before all of this happened?"

"He wouldn't! His father would . . . " She shook herself. "I mean to say, Emmett's a good boy! Obedient!"

"Cody and Mina are gone, too," Canna said. "I went to their rooms when the shooting started, and their beds were also empty!"

Hazel Scott gasped, elbowing her way to them though her daughters attempted to hold her back. "Albert! He ain't home neither! I feared he'd gone t' the stable t' see the foaling, and they'd done got him when they . . . when they . . . when they kill't Abram . . . but mebbe . . . ?"

In that moment, despite their differences, all three mothers were one.

"Now, Hazel," Mr. Scott began, in a don't-git-yer-hopes-up tone he lacked the strength to sustain. Rather than continue, he had to turn away, struggling mightily to contain his emotions.

A general murmur spiraled toward babble. Then the woman in black, the carnival's **Deadly Lotus**, cut through it as if even her words were a sword.

"Your children," she said clearly. "I know where they are."

Albert couldn't stop touching his ear. Tried to do it subtle-like, when no one was looking, not wanting to draw even more attention.

It wasn't as if Emmett weren't doing the same with his leg, pressing at it through the cloth of the too-large borrowed pants someone had brung him. The pants hid the place where the arrow had stuck, though they'd all seen the wound. Yet, here he was, up and walking.

Similar for Cody, too; Cody kept rocking his head back and forth, rolling it on his neck, turning it this way and that, as if surprised it still worked right. Surprised it didn't hurt anymore. After the knock he'd taken, a knock that would've stunned an ox!

No one would find it strange, then, if Albert's hand kept straying up.

Mina'd told him about Emmett's healing, what she'd seen, what they'd done. He'd experienced it himself when they did the same for him, though he'd been tempted to pass it off as some effect of whatever medicine it was Rainbow Annie had given him.

No reg'lar medicine could account for this.

He touched his ear again.

It felt not-quite-right, weird and misshapen. The one glimpse he'd had of it in Rainbow Annie's mirror showed him a brownish-pink crinkle of tissue stuck to a blotchy patch of what looked like partly-melted wax. His hair might not grow back fully around the spot, they'd told him. He'd forever have the scar. His hearing—which, right now on that side, was as if stuffed with cotton—might get better, or it might not.

But, his *ear*!

Shredded to bits by those claws! Raking so deep they'd scraped his skull-bone! Blood fair to pouring all down his shoulder! He shouldn't ought to have lived. Or, should have lived only a while at best, as it festered, as infection set in, and he swelled up the side of his head bullfrog-bloated full of pus, until it rotted clear through to his brain.

Here he was, though. Because the **Living Ghost** had set those oh-so-white hands to him and eased the worst of the injury away. Here he was, also sitting in borrowed too-large clothes, at a long plank table in a big carnival tent. Him, Cody, Emmett, Mina, Saleel, and freckle-faced Iain whose name they finally knew.

Sitting with **Tom Short**, who for as gruff as he'd come across earlier, took to Albert like another uncle—"Us coloreds gotta stick together, whatever our size, eh, am I right?" he'd said, flashing Albert a grin. Sitting with the fancy-man, and Rainbow Annie, who seemed to be the fancy-man's lady. And **Doctor Oddico** himself, who seemed to be the fancy-man's father.

The **Living Ghost**, however, was not in attendance. Healings took their toll. **Mother Sybil** also must have been resting. **Princess Crow-Feather** had passed the dog to Mina with some hasty explanation of being needed elsewhere. Something to do with her birds, though Albert hadn't seen a single crow since they reached the camp.

Other carnival-folk went to and fro, and for all it was well past midnight, served up a fine meal, and made their guests welcome with every hospitality. Beds had been offered, but sleep was the furthest thing from their minds. They listened—even Albert with his magic-healed ear—as Mina finally got some of her many questions answered.

They were all, **Doctor Oddico** said, deeply regretful and bitter sorry for what had happened earlier in the evening. *Mother Sybil*, it seemed, had known of their presence as soon as they'd sneaked near to the camp. Was not the first time adventuresome townies had done such, wouldn't be the last. Was, in their eyes, part of the fun.

So they'd done what they usually did, acted as if nothing were the least bit unusual, gone to their wagons, waiting to see how bold they'd be. Which then, of course, Cody went and urged them to have a closer look, to try and see some of the advertised oddities.

"The jawbones of an ancient, giant breed of shark," **Doctor Oddico** told them when they asked what those monstrous *teeth* that so scared them had been.

"We oughtn't have laughed," his son the fancy-man said, sounding proper remorseful. Then he winked. "But . . . it *was* pretty funny, the way you all screamed."

"I oughtn't have yelled," added **Tom Short**. "Only a joke, meant to give you another jump, just in fun."

"Nor'd we expect ye take off runnin' so fast." Rainbow Annie chimed in.

That was when, in an effort to learn if they were all right, **Mother Sybil** had . . . well, Albert didn't quite understand *what* she had done. Only that she'd known they were in terrible, mortal danger. Right quick, the decision had been made to send help.

Princess Crow-Feather's winged friends served as scouts—

"They argued, remember?" Mina said. "Crow or nighthawk or whatever, he'd buy them a bird-book?"

—while the ***Man-Mountain, Deadly Lotus***, and a volunteer posse of roustabouts set out on the rescue.

"What about the ***Blind Bandito***?" Cody made double-fisted gunslinger gestures. "Isn't he with you? And why didn't the others come back to camp?"

Doctor Oddico removed his nose-pinch spectacles and rubbed the spot where they gripped. He sighed in a way that Albert—that *every* kid—knew indicated a grown-up who had to say something they wouldn't like to hear.

Saleel, who'd re-tied the black band around her throat and not spoken since giving them Iain's name, got a stricken look. As if, whatever the foreboding news might be, she'd already guessed.

Emmett also must've reached some similar conclusion, because he sat up straight. "The bad guys," he said. "They mentioned a boss. A boss who was . . . clear on the other side of town . . . "

"There are more of them!" Cody sprang to his feet. "More than we saw just at Ol' Man Starkey's place! A whole gang of outlaws, attacking Silver River! We gotta—"

"'T' wait here with us, laddie-o," Rainbow Annie said.

"But—" Mina was on her feet, too; the dog yipped as she anxiously clutched it tight.

"Your homes, your families, I know," ***Doctor Oddico*** said.

The fancy-man nodded. "Even if there were anything you could do, by the time you'd get there—"

"So what? We can't just sit here!" Cody twitched from Rainbow Annie's tattooed, placating hand. "We have to *try*!"

"They'd want you to be safe," said **Tom Short**. "Those we've sent, they're our best. Seen some of that for yourselfs already, yeah? Let them do what they do."

Hadn't taken much more than a cursory survey to convince him he might as well make himself scarce.

Particularly with Nate dead.

No Nate Bast, no Nasty Bastards. Even if the dregs of the gang somehow did escape and hold together, well . . . Horsecock knew how most of them felt about him.

Their attentions being diverted and all, it was simple enough to slip over to his trusty Blondie, mount up, and ride.

He'd got what he needed here, anyways. Time to move on. There were always other towns. Other husbands who could stand to be taught a lesson, and other wives who deserved to know if they had a real man.

The full moon sank lower in the west, as if exhausted by all it had seen in its course across the sky.

Once the shooting had stopped, neighbors from the outer-lying farms and homesteads dared venture to see what, if anything, was left of the town. Mr. Cottonwood sent armed ranch-hands to patrol the valley, dispatching urgent messages to the fort and Winston City. Several Truthers came down from Highwell, and stayed to offer what aid as they could.

At Lost Meadow, parents and children were reunited. Tears were shed, both of grief and relief, but no whippings were administered.

There were losses to be mourned, dead to be buried, a great deal of clean-up to be done. For many, the horrors would never be overcome. To rebuild or abandon yet remained to be seen.

The future hung uncertain, but the eastern sky brightened toward dawn, finally bringing an end to the night Silver River run red.

ABOUT THE AUTHOR

Christine Morgan grew up in the high deserts of Southern California, surrounded by Joshua Trees, breathtaking rugged scenery, annual poppy blooms, and spectacular sunsets. And wind. And gritty dust. And tumbleweeds. And heat. And wildfires.

And she fucking hated it. Despite having a history-nut dad whose idea of the perfect family vacation was a trip to Calico or Bodie ghost towns, and a photographer mom who couldn't get enough of Bryce Canyon and Vasquez Rocks, she moved to the cool and damp coastal northwest as soon as she was of age.

Her favorite western movies/shows include *Silverado, Deadwood, The Adventures of Brisco County Jr.,* and a ridiculous affection for *Wild, Wild West,* partly because the abovementioned history-nut dad got to be an extra in it. The scene where the amphibious steampunk tank-thing trundles ashore? See the tall Confederate soldier with a hat and a full silver beard who hunkers down to look at the treads? That's him.

Being scared of horses and sudden loud noises,

she'd make a terrible gunslinger. She does love the language, the lore, and the larger-than-life legendariness of the genre, though. She also sometimes suspects she was a frontier brothel madam in a past life. Writing this book was the absolute most fun she's had with any project except maybe for *Lakehouse Infernal*.